TRISTANA

BENITO PÉREZ GALDÓS (1843–1920) was born into a
middle-class family in Las Palmas in the Canary Islands.
When he was nineteen, he was sent to Madrid to study law.
Once there, however, he neglected his studies and plunged
into the ordinary life of the capital, an experience that both
developed his social and political conscience and confirmed
him in his vocation as a writer. He became an assiduous
theater- and concert-goer and a visitor to galleries and
museums, and began publishing articles on literature, art,
music, and politics. Galdós was the first to translate *The
Pickwick Papers* into Spanish, and on a visit to Paris, discovered
the works of Balzac. His first novel, *La fontana de oro*, was
published privately and initially met with little interest. It
wasn't long, though, before critics were hailing it as a new
beginning for the Spanish novel. In a career that spanned
more than forty years, Galdós wrote nearly eighty novels and
some twenty plays. He also managed to find time to travel
widely, in Spain and abroad, and to conduct a series of
discreet affairs—one of them with fellow novelist Emilia
Pardo Bazán. Perhaps his most ambitious literary project,
entitled *Episodios nacionales*, comprised forty-six books, each
chronicling a different episode in Spanish history from the
Battle of Trafalgar onward. He continued to write until his
death at the age of seventy-six, dictating his novels to an
amanuensis when blindness overtook him. Galdós provides
his readers with an extraordinarily vivid picture of life in

nineteenth-century Spain; his novels teem with fascinating characters from all social classes. His masterpiece is generally considered to be the vast and wonderful *Fortunata and Jacinta*, but equally impressive are such works as *Doña Perfecta*, *Misericordia*, *La de Bringas*, and *Miau*. Luis Buñuel based three of his movies— *Viridiana*, *Nazarín*, and *Tristana*—on three Galdós novels, perhaps recognizing in Galdós a fellow subversive.

MARGARET JULL COSTA has been a translator of Spanish and Portuguese literature for nearly thirty years. Among the authors she has translated are José Saramago, Javier Marías, and Eça de Queiroz. She has won many prizes, including the PEN Translation Prize. In 2013 she was invited to become a Fellow of the Royal Society of Literature, and in 2014 she was awarded an OBE for her services to literature. She lives in the United Kingdom.

JEREMY TREGLOWN is a writer and literary critic known most recently for his work on Spanish culture, film, and literature. His books include several biographies, including *V. S. Pritchett*, which was short-listed for the Whitbread Award for Biography, and most recently *Franco's Crypt: Spanish Culture and Memory Since 1936*. He was the editor of *The Times Literary Supplement* for almost a decade and is currently the Donald C. Gallup Fellow in American Literature at the Beinecke Library at Yale. He lives in the United Kingdom.

TRISTANA

BENITO PÉREZ GALDÓS

Translated from the Spanish by
MARGARET JULL COSTA

Introduction by
JEREMY TREGLOWN

NEW YORK REVIEW BOOKS

New York

THIS IS A NEW YORK REVIEW BOOK
PUBLISHED BY THE NEW YORK REVIEW OF BOOKS
435 Hudson Street, New York, NY 10014
www.nyrb.com

Library of Congress Cataloging-in-Publication Data
Pérez Galdós, Benito, 1843–1920.
[Tristana. English]
 Tristana / by Benito Pérez Galdós ; translated by Margaret Jull Costa ;
introduction by Jeremy Treglown.
    pages cm — (New York Review Books classics)
 ISBN 978-1-59017-765-5 (alk. paper)
 I. Costa, Margaret Jull, translator. II. Title.
PQ6555.T813 2014
863'.5—dc23

                      2014020926

ISBN 978-1-59017-765-5
Available as an electronic book; ISBN 978-1-59017-792-1

Printed in the United States of America on acid-free paper.
10 9 8 7 6 5 4 3 2 1

INTRODUCTION

WITHIN a few pages, two people have taken over our imaginations. In some ways their predicaments are formulaic: an aging, self-mythologizing, predatory yet generous man lives with an attractive, passionate, much younger woman who is beginning to sense her separate potential. We're warned early on that although people feel themselves to be unique and complex, their specialness is generally "an amalgamation . . . of the ideas floating around in the metaphysical atmosphere of the age, like . . . invisible bacteria." This is part of what makes *Tristana* a novel of the late nineteenth century rather than just a folktale. The story will be ironic; it will be about the ordinary illusion of specialness, yet it will also reinforce that illusion.

From the outset, matters seem unlikely to end well. "Socially" speaking—in the terms of Henry James, say—Tristana's position is not so much ambiguous as scarcely mentionable. Benito Pérez Galdós was James's exact contemporary and understood his society no less well than James did his own, but this isn't a novel by James or about his world, and its ironies are more robust. Tristana, we're told in the riddling way of a folktale, "was neither daughter, niece, or wife" to Don Lope, but "she belonged to him." Here, the always fluid narrative viewpoint is that of local gossip. She belongs to him, people say, like "a tobacco pouch," and if that's a double entendre, so it's probably meant to be. Tristana isn't just a receptacle, though, nor is she *nada*, which people also say about her. Galdós liked women—really liked them, as individuals—and his novels are keenly alert to what it was to be them. It's striking how many of his stories have women's names. *Tristana* was published in 1892 and by then every Western reader knew *Madame Bovary* and *Anna Karenina*, but those are about married women who have taken their husband's names. Few of the great pre-twentieth-century fictions written by men take their titles unequivocally from a heroine (*Pamela* is an exception; *Evelina* and *Emma* are by women writers; *Eugénie Grandet* and *Thérèse Raquin* come close but are so called because of the different kinds of power the heroines' eponymous fathers and cousins have over them). Yet Galdós wrote *Marianela* (1878) and *Fortunata and Jacinta* (1887) as well as *Tristana*, and the third of these shows signs of wanting to become a feminist work. Its "substance," according to one contemporary critic, is "the wakening of the consciousness of a woman who rebels against a society that condemns her to everlasting shame, and is incapable of offering her a respectable way of earning her living." The reviewer was Spain's first important woman novelist and first woman academic, Emilia Pardo Bazán. As it happens, she and Galdós had not long before ended a love affair, so she may be assumed to have read the story with particular interest. He was forty-nine, the same age at which his roué hero's counting of the years "stuck fast . . . as if an instinctive terror of the number fifty had halted him on the much-feared boundary of the half century." Don Lope is fifty-seven when the book opens, and both he and, increasingly, Tristana realize that whether or not his arithmetic is stuck, he won't get any younger. But aging isn't mathematically regulated, and in Tristana's case it will be violently accelerated by illness and surgery.

How the reader interprets this disabling misfortune to a large extent determines how the book is understood and evaluated. Pardo Bazán and, following her, some recent critics have seen it as at best an arbitrary way of moving the plot along, at worst a peculiarly male kind of fictional revenge on a woman for daring to be free (Tristana's romance with Horacio begins, after all, on one of the long *walks* she used to take with the maid, Saturna, despite the crude old Spanish proverb that said 'A woman's place is at home with a broken leg'). In life, though, illness and disability do afflict people and alter their relationships, and generally in ways that seem to have no meaning.

Galdós's plotting may be rough-and-ready, but it's all too real. Among the realities that concern him is the role played in life by luck.

We're nudged by the backstory into wondering where things began to go wrong for Tristana (does her name imply something essentially sad in her?), or for any of the other characters. Like most women in her world, she has been given next to no education—this even though her mother, Josefina, had literary ambitions. Her father, Antonio, was unlucky with money; only Don Lope's generosity saved the family from ruin. Released from prison, the demoralized Antonio soon dies, and his widow falls victim to what would now be called an obsessive-compulsive disorder. (How vividly madness draws out Galdós's always observant sympathy.) Josefina dies, too, handing her daughter over to Don Lope to look after—a responsibility that he abuses, and not only in today's terms. The narrative asserts, albeit in Galdós's dry, hard-to-gauge way, that Don Lope's "moral sense lacked a vital component, and like some terribly mutilated organ, it functioned only partially and suffered frequent deplorable breakdowns." We hear about this *mutilación* long before Tristana is operated on, but it seems relevant that the same word is used then.

Others have been unlucky, too. Saturna's husband was killed in a workplace accident, so she became Don Lope's servant and put her son into institutional care, along with children born blind or deaf, whose plights Galdós again dwells on. (Luis Buñuel makes more of this boy in his powerful, very free film adaptation.) Don Lope endures the consequences of the liberality he seems to have been born with, and which is one of his more appealing traits. Yet this is no victim culture. Under siege from her sexually remorseless guardian, Tristana—who is in her early twenties—nonetheless finds "moments of brief, pale happiness, tiny hints of what the pleasures of love might be." She will experience them more fully with Horacio. Shocked when she wakes up to the situation she's in, she's also realistic about it: honest both about her seducer's good qualities and about the extent to which her problems derive from her upbringing and the values of her society. And while she's a fantasist, she's also pragmatic: enterprising and independent in her outings to different parts of Madrid; quick to make the most of her affair with Horacio; brave in physical adversity. If anyone is self-pitying here, it's the rich young artist to whose tales about his dreadful upbringing Tristana listens so eagerly. Horacio is the eligible man who can't or won't commit, which is lucky, in a way, given that commitment is something Tristana doesn't want.

Now everything seems to fall apart and this is where the novel may, but shouldn't, disappoint—loose though the author's handling of its elements briefly becomes. Horacio goes off to the Mediterranean with his aunt and on both sides the affair with Tristana turns for a time into a solipsistic fantasy buoyed up on a flood of letters. Then she becomes ill and when she and Horacio next meet . . . but an introduction ought not to give away too much. Perhaps it's better to put forth some questions. Is the way things go now between Horacio and Tristana implausible? Does Horacio behave badly? What about the by now increasingly vulnerable Don Lope, and the new turns taken by Tristana's ambitiousness, and above all about how she and Don Lope fetch up? The most explicit question is asked by the novel itself, at the end. It's about the two characters both as individuals and together—*uno y otro*—but also implicitly it's about how much we think any human narrative can or should tell us. Galdós's answer is: "Perhaps"—"*Tal vez*."

Literally, the Spanish words mean "such a time." This isn't how they should be translated but, to see the problem the other way around, a Spanish person reading "perhaps" might not know that in English the word carries distant memories of *hap*, meaning chance, as in "mishap" and also, strangely, "happiness." Almost subliminally, for a Spanish writer to isolate *tal vez* like this can be seen as subtly heightening the story's ponderings on the passage of time, on aging, on lost pasts and imagined futures: Tristana's exuberant dreams of freedom, of becoming an actor, a painter, a musician, a saint; Don Lope's quixotic regrets for a more gallant past, all those "rare muskets and rusty harquebuses, pistols, halberds, Moorish and Christian flintlocks, hilted swords, breastplates and backplates" which decorated his walls but which, in another part of himself and in the today of that part of the novel, he knows have no value except the money they can raise to help his friend, Tristana's father. "One has what one has," he believes, "until someone else needs it."

Mainly, "perhaps" throws out the happily-after-after hopes associated with a folktale as well as the more pessimistic certainties associated with nineteenth-century realism. Admitted, those certainties are less than they've been claimed to be, whether by their proponents—especially a bit before Galdós, Henrik Ibsen, and Émile Zola—or by modern cultural historians. The fictive ironies that critics have more justly drawn attention to in all of Galdós's work are present in *Tristana* long before its ending. He's not a modernist novelist, but he is a transitional one and he expects us to do some work while he enjoys himself. Part of that is not making every decision for us. Don Lope is a bad man, but he's also a good one. Well, which is he? The novelist's shrug is nowhere more satirically vigorous than during a passage about the old bachelor's self-serving opinions on "the man-woman relationship" and the urgent need for a repeal of the Mosaic law in relation to it. "Needless to say," the narrator says, "all those who knew [him], myself included, abominate such ideas and wholeheartedly deplore the fact that this foolish gentleman's conduct proved to be such a faithful application of his perverse doctrines. It should be added that among those of us who value the major principles that form the basis ... etcetera, etcetera ..., it makes our hair stand on end just to think what the social machine would be like if its enlightened operators took it into their heads to ..."

"*Etcétera, etcétera*"! It's as teasing as the blank page in *Tristram Shandy*. Galdós is a really funny writer and this, along with "perhaps," is a crucial element in *Tristana*'s seriousness, and its sadness.

—JEREMY TREGLOWN

TRISTANA

I

IN THE populous quarter of Chamberí, toward the water tower end rather than Cuatro Caminos, there lived, not so many years ago, an agreeable-looking gentleman with a most unusual name, and he lived not in an ancestral mansion—for there are none in that part of town—but in a cheap, plebeian rented room, with, as noisy neighbors, a tavern, a café, a shop selling milk fresh from the goat, and a narrow inner courtyard with numbered rooms. The first time I encountered this gentleman and observed his proud, soldierly bearing, like a figure in a Velázquez painting of one of Spain's regiments in Flanders, I was informed that his name was Don Lope de Sosa, a name with more than a whiff of the theater about it* and worthy of a character in one of those short tales you find in books on rhetoric; and that, indeed, was the name given to him by some of his more unsavory friends; he, however, answered to Don Lope Garrido.† In time, I discovered that the name on his baptismal certificate was Don Juan López Garrido; so that sonorous Don Lope must have been his own invention, like a lovely ornament intended to embellish his person; and the name so suited the firm, noble lines of his lean face, his slim, erect body, his slightly hooked nose, his clear brow and lively eyes, his graying mustache and neat, provocative goatee, that he really could not have been called anything else. One had no alternative but to call him Don Lope.

---

*A reference to the great Golden Age playwright Lope de Vega.
†"Garrido" can mean handsome and elegant but carries, too, a suggestion of *garras*: claws.

The age of this excellent gentleman, in terms of the figure he gave whenever the subject came up, was a number as impossible to verify as the time on a broken clock, whose hands refuse to move. He had stuck fast at forty-nine, as if an instinctive terror of the number fifty had halted him on the much-feared boundary of the half century; but not even all-powerful God could have taken from him the fifty-seven years, which, however well he wore them, were no less real for all that. He dressed as smartly and impeccably as his slender means permitted: a well-buffed top hat, a good-quality winter cape, dark gloves at every season of the year, an elegant cane in summer, and suits more appropriate to youth than to maturity. Don Lope Garrido—just to whet your appetite—was a skilled strategist in the war of love and prided himself on having stormed more bastions of virtue and captured more strongholds of chastity than he had hairs on his head. True, he was somewhat spent now and not fit for very much, but he could never quite give up that saucy hobby of his, and whenever he passed a pretty woman, or even a plain one, he would draw himself up and, albeit with no evil intentions, shoot her a meaningful glance, more paternal than mischievous, as if to say: "You had a very narrow escape! Think yourself lucky you weren't born twenty years earlier. Beware any men who were as I once was, although, if pressed, I would say that there are no men today who could equal me in my prime. Nowadays, men or, perish the thought, gallants, young and old alike, simply don't know how to behave in the company of a beautiful woman."

With no profession, good Don Lope, had, in happier times, enjoyed a modest fortune, though all that remained of this was some property in Toledo, which provided him with an ever-decreasing income, and he now spent his time either in idle, agreeable chatter at his club or else methodically doing the rounds of his friends, meeting up with them in cafés or centers—perhaps a better word would be "dark corners"—of pleasure that need not be named here. The only reason he lived in such an out-of-the-way place was the cheapness of the accommodation, which, even with the added expense of the tram fare, was very reasonable indeed, and there were other benefits too: the better light, the fresher air, and the broad, smiling horizon. Not that Garrido was a night owl: he was up each morning at eight, and it took him two whole hours to shave and generally spruce himself up, for he took the same kind of meticulous, leisurely care over his appearance as might a man of the world. He spent the rest of the morning out and about until one o'clock, when he promptly partook of a frugal lunch. He then resumed his peregrinations until seven or eight in the evening, at which hour he ate a no less sober supper, whose sparseness even the most elementary of culinary arts could ill disguise. One thing we should point out is that while Don Lope was all affability and politeness at, for example, the café or his club, at home, he blended courteous but colloquial language with the indisputable authority of the master.

With him lived two women, one a maid, the other a lady, at least in name, for they worked together in the kitchen and performed the same simple household tasks, with no hierarchical differences and in perfect, sisterly camaraderie, a relationship determined more by the abasement of the lady than by any conceit on the part of the maid. The latter's name was Saturna, and she was tall and thin, with dark eyes, rather mannish in appearance and, having recently been widowed, dressed in deepest mourning. The recent loss of her husband—a bricklayer who had fallen while working on the scaffolding where the new Bank was being built—had meant that she could put her son in the local hospice for children of the poor and find employment as a maid, her first job being in Don Lope's house —hardly an outpost in the Land of Plenty. The other woman— whom one would sometimes assume to be a servant and sometimes not, for she sat at the table with the master and addressed him informally as *tú*—was young, pretty, and slender, and her skin was the almost implausible white of pure alabaster; she had the palest of cheeks and dark eyes more notable for their vivacity and brightness than for their size; her remarkable eyebrows looked as if they had been drawn with the tip of the very finest of brushes; her delicate mouth, with its rather plump, round lips, was so red it seemed to contain all the blood that her face lacked; her small teeth were like pieces of concentrated crystal; her hair, caught up in a graceful tangle on the top of her head, was brown and very fine, and had the sheen of plaited silk. This singular creature's most marked characteristic, however, was her ermine-white purity and cleanliness, for she remained unsoiled by even the most indelicate of household chores. Her perfect hands—ah, what hands!—had a mysterious quality, as did her body and her clothes, which seemed to announce to the lower orders of the physical world: *La vostra miseria non mi tange*.* Everything about her gave the impression of an intrinsic, elemental cleanliness that had been spared all contact with things unclean or impure. When she was in her ordinary clothes, with chamois leather in hand, the dust and dirt somehow respected her; and when she put on her purple dressing gown adorned with white rosettes, with her hair in a chignon pierced by gold-tipped pins, she was the very image of an aristocratic Japanese lady—what else?—given that she seemed entirely made out of paper, the same warm, flexible, living paper on which those inspired Oriental artists painted the divine and the human, the seriously comical and the comically serious. Her matte white face was made of paper, as were her dress and her fine, shapely, incomparable hands.

We should, at this point, explain the relationship between Tristana—for that was the lovely girl's name—and the great Don Lope, lord and master of that henhouse, since it would be wrong to view them as a family. In the neighborhood, and among the few people who dropped in to visit or to snoop, there was a theory to suit every taste, and the various theories put forth on this important matter were, variously, either in fashion or out. For a period of about two or three months, it was held to be the gospel truth that the young lady was Don Lope's niece. Then a contrary view—that she was his daughter—took hold, and there were even some who claimed to have heard her say "Papa," just like one of those talking dolls. After which another opinion blew in, according to which she was none other than Don Lope's legal wife. More time passed and these

---

*"Your suffering does not touch me": from Dante's *Inferno*, canto 2, line 92.

vain conjectures vanished without a trace, and in the view of the surrounding populace, Tristana was neither daughter, niece, or wife, in fact, she was no relation of the great Don Lope's at all; she was nothing, and that was all there was to it, for she belonged to him as if she were a tobacco pouch, an item of furniture, or an article of clothing, with no one to dispute his ownership; and she seemed perfectly resigned to being nothing but a tobacco pouch!

2

WELL, not entirely resigned, no, because every now and then, in the year prior to the one we will be describing here, that pretty little paper doll would stamp her feet in an attempt to show that she had the character and consciousness of a free woman. Her master ruled over her with a despotism one might term "seductive," imposing his will on her with tender authority, even, sometimes, with cuddles and caresses, thus destroying in her all initiative, apart from that required for incidental, unimportant things. She was twenty-one when, along with the doubts filling her mind about her very strange social situation, there awoke in her a desire for independence. When this process began, she still had the behavior and habits of a child; her eyes did not know how to look to the future, or if they did, they saw nothing. But one day, she noticed the shadow that her present life cast on all future spaces, and that image of herself, as a distorted, broken shadow stretching into the distance, occupied her mind for a long time, suggesting a thousand troubling, confusing thoughts.

In order to understand Tristana's anxieties, we need to shed more light on Don Lope, so that you do not judge him to be either better or worse than he actually was. He believed that he was practicing, in all its dogmatic purity, the art of being a gentleman, or perhaps a knight, of the sedentary rather than the errant variety, but he interpreted the laws of that religion with excessive freedom, producing a very complex morality, which, despite being very much his own, was also quite widespread, the abundant fruit of the times we live in; a morality which, although it seemed to have sprung solely from him, was, in fact, an amalgamation in his mind of the ideas floating around in the metaphysical atmosphere of the age, like the invisible bacteria that inhabit the physical atmosphere. As an external phenomenon, Don Lope's knightliness was obvious to everyone: he never took anything that was not his, and when it came to money matters, he carried his delicacy to quixotic extremes. He dealt gracefully with his penurious state and disguised it with consummate dignity, giving frequent proof of self-abnegation and stoically condemning materialistic appetites. For him, money was never anything more than base metal and, as such, merited the scorn of any wellborn person, regardless of the joy that might be gained from earning it. The ease with which money slipped through his fingers was further evidence of this disdain, far more convincing, indeed, than his vituperations against what he judged to be the root of all evil and the reason why there were now so few true gentlemen. As regards personal decorum, he was so meticulous, his susceptibilities so easily bruised, that he would not tolerate the most insignificant of slights or ambiguities of language that might contain within them the merest hint of disrespect. He had fought many a duel in his time, and so keen was he to maintain the laws governing a man's personal dignity that he became a living rule book on affairs of honor, and if anyone had any doubts about the intricate etiquette of dueling, the great Don Lope would be consulted and he would opine and pronounce with priestly authority, as if he were giving his opinion on an important theological or philosophical problem.

The point of honor was, for Don Lope, the be-all and end-all of the science of living, which he rounded off with a series of totally conflicting views. While his disinterestedness might be considered a virtue, his scorn for the State and for Justice, as human organisms, could not. He loathed the legal profession, and as for the footling employees of the tax office, who stood between the institutions and the taxpayer with outstretched hand, he believed them to be suitable fodder for the galleys. In an age in which paper ruled rather than steel, an age overrun with empty formulae, he deplored the fact that gentlemen were no longer allowed to carry a sword with them in order to deal with those throngs of impertinent good-for-nothings.

Society, he believed, had created various mechanisms whose sole object was to support mere idlers and to persecute and rob wellborn gentlefolk.

Given these beliefs, Don Lope was wholeheartedly in favor of smugglers and thieves, and had it been in his power, he would definitely have sided with them in a tight spot. He hated the police, both secret and uniformed, and heaped insults on guards and customs officers alike, as well as those half-wits in charge of "public order," who, in his opinion, never protected the weak from the strong. He tolerated the civil guard, although he—damn it—would have organized them quite differently, giving the members legal and executive powers, as knights of the one true religion on the highways and byways of the land. As for the army, Don Lope's ideas verged on the eccentric. As he saw it, the army was merely a political instrument, one that was both stupid and costly to boot, whereas it should, in his view, be a religious and military organization, like the old knightly orders, drawn from the people, with service being obligatory and with hereditary leaders, generalships being handed down from father to son, in short, such a complex, labyrinthine system that not even he could understand it. As regards the church, he thought it was little more than a bad joke played by the past on the present, which society was too timid or stupid to reject. Not that he was irreligious; on the contrary, his faith was far stronger than that of many who go sniffing around altars and clinging to the skirts of the priests. The ingenious Don Lope had no time for the latter at all, because he could find no place for them in the pseudo-knightly system concocted by his idle imagination; he used to say: "We are the true priests, we who watch over honor and morality, we who fight for the innocent, we, the enemies of evil, hypocrisy, and injustice . . . and base metal."

There had been episodes in this man's life that would have exalted him in a high degree, and had anyone—with nothing better to do—decided to write his biography, those glowing examples of generosity and self-denial would have helped obscure, up to a point, the darker side of his character and conduct. And we should speak of these, as the antecedents and causes of what we will describe in due course. Don Lope was always a very good friend to his friends, a man who would do anything to help loved ones who found themselves in desperate straits. Helpful to the point of heroism, he put no limits on his generous impulses. His knightliness verged on vanity, and vanity always has a price—just as the luxury of good intentions is always the most expensive—and Don Lope's fortunes suffered as a result. His family motto, "Give your shirt to your friend," was not a mere rhetorical affectation. He may not have given his shirt, but he had often, like Saint Martin, given half his cloak away, and quite recently, his shirt—that most useful of items because closest to our skin—had been at grave risk.

A childhood friend, whom he loved dearly, Don Antonio Reluz by name, a comrade in certain more or less respectable acts of chivalry, put good Don Lope's altruistic fervor—for that is what it was—fully to the test. When Reluz fell in love with and married a very distinguished young lady, he rejected his friend's knightly ideas and practices, judging that they neither constituted a profession nor put food on the table, and so he devoted himself to investing his wife's meager capital in profitable business deals. He did quite well the first few years. He became involved in the buying and selling of barley, in contracts for military supplies, and other such honest trades, upon which Garrido looked down with lofty disdain. Around 1880, when both had crossed over into their fifties, Reluz's star suddenly waned, and every deal he made went bad on him. In the end, he was laid low by a faithless colleague, a treacherous friend, and overnight that blow left him penniless, dishonored, and, worse still, in prison.

"You see!" Don Lope said. "Now are you convinced that you and I are not made to be mere hawkers? I warned you at the start, but you took no notice. We don't belong in the modern age, dear Antonio, we are too decent to be involved in such dealings. Leave them to the rabble."

These were not the most consoling of words, and Reluz listened without blinking, saying nothing, wondering how and when he would fire the bullet with which he intended to put an end to his unbearable suffering.

Garrido was quick to respond, and immediately offered to make the supreme sacrifice of his shirt.

"To save your honor, I would give you the . . . Besides, you know that this is not a matter of favors, but of duty; we are true friends, and what I do for you, you would do for me."

Although the debts that had muddied Reluz's good name hardly amounted to a king's ransom, they were enough to demolish the rather shaky edifice of Don Lope's very small fortune, for Don Lope, entrenched in his altruistic dogma, did the decent, manly thing, and sold off first a small property he had in Toledo, then his collection of old paintings, which were not perhaps of the first order, but whose value lay in the hours of pleasure and amusement they represented.

"Don't worry," he said to his sad friend. "Stand firm in the face of misfortune and, besides, I have done nothing of particular merit. In these putrescent times, people treat the most basic of obligations as if they were displays of virtue. One has what one has, until someone else needs it. That is the law that governs human relationships, and the rest is nothing but egotism and mercenariness. Base metal only ceases to be base when one offers it to someone who has the misfortune to need it. I have no children. Take what I have: we won't go without our crust of bread."

Needless to say, Reluz was deeply moved to hear these words. And he never did fire that bullet; he had no reason to, for alas, no sooner had he left prison and returned home than he caught a vicious fever that carried him off in a matter of days. It was doubtless brought on by his feelings of gratitude and by the terrible emotions he had been through. He left behind him an inconsolable widow— who tried very hard to follow him to the grave *by a natural death*, but failed—and a daughter of only nineteen, called Tristana.

3

RELUZ'S widow had been very pretty before all this upset and commotion. However, the aging process was not so quick and clear that it dimmed Don Lope's desire to court her, for although his knightly code forbade him from wooing the wife of a living friend, the death of that friend left him free to apply, as he saw fit, the law of love. Nevertheless, as fate would have it, things did not turn out well, because when he uttered his first tender words to the inconsolable widow, her response was far from expected and it became clear that her mind was not working as it should; in short, poor Josefina Solís lacked many of the mental mechanisms necessary for good judgment and sensible action. She was tormented in particular by two of the thousands of obsessions besieging her mind: moving house and cleanliness. Each week or, at least, each month, she would summon the removal carts, who made a small fortune that year traipsing her goods and chattels around all the streets and squares in Madrid. Every house was magnificent on the day they moved in and detestable, inhospitable, and vile a week later. In this house she nearly froze to death, while in that one she roasted; this house was plagued by noisy neighbors and another by the most brazen of mice; and every house contained the longing for somewhere else, for the removals cart, an infinite desire for the unknown.

Don Lope tried to put a stop to this costly madness, but soon saw that it was impossible. Josefina spent the brief time between moves washing and scrubbing everything in sight, driven by nervous scruples and feelings of profound disgust, far stronger than the most powerful, instinctive impulse. She would shake no one by the hand, afraid that she might catch shingles or some kind of repugnant pustule. She ate only eggs, having first washed the shell, but even these she ate very warily for fear that the hen who had laid them might have been pecking at something impure. A fly sent her wild with panic. She would dismiss the maids at a moment's notice for some innocent contravention of her eccentric cleaning methods. It wasn't enough that she ruined the furniture with water and scouring, she also washed the rugs, the spring mattresses, and even the piano inside and out. She surrounded herself with disinfectants and antiseptics, and even the food they ate smelled faintly of camphor. If I tell you that she washed the clocks, I need say no more. She plunged her daughter in the bathtub three times a day, and the cat fled in disgust, unable to bear the washing regimen imposed on him by his mistress.

Don Lope regretted his friend's mental decay with all his heart and missed the sweet, kind Josefina of former days, for she had been a pleasant, rather well-educated person, who even fancied herself a woman of letters. In private, she wrote poetry, which she showed only to her closest friends, and she displayed unusual discernment when it came to literature and contemporary authors. By temperament, upbringing, and atavism—two of her uncles were members of the Academy and another had fled to London with the romantic poets Duque de Rivas and Alcalá Galiano—she hated the realist trend in literature and worshipped idealism and the fine, beautifully turned phrase. She firmly believed that when it came to taste, there was the aristocratic and the plebeian, and she did not hesitate to assign herself a very obscure little corner among the most eminent writers. She loved the old plays, and knew by heart entire speeches from *Don Gil of the Green Breeches*, *The Suspicious Truth*, and *The Prodigious Magician*.* She had a son, who died when he was twelve, and whom she called Lisardo, as if he were a character out of a play by Tirso de Molino or Agustín Moreto. Her daughter owed her name, Tristana, to her mother's passion for the noble, chivalrous art

---

*Golden Age plays by, respectively, Tirso de Molina, Juan Ruíz de Alarcón, and Pedro Calderón de la Barca.

of the theater, which created an ideal society to serve as a constant model and example to our own crude, vulgar realities.

However, the refined tastes that once so embellished her character, thus adding even more charm to her natural graces, vanished without a trace. In her crazed obsession with moving house and with cleanliness, Josefina forgot all about her past. Her memory, like a tarnished mirror, preserved not a single idea, name, or phrase from the fictional world she had so loved. One day, Don Lope tried to remind the unfortunate lady of her past, but saw only blank ignorance on her face, as if he were speaking to her of some previous life. She understood nothing, could remember nothing, and did not even know who Pedro Calderón was, thinking at first that he was perhaps a house agent or the owner of the removal carts. On another occasion, he found her washing her slippers, with, beside her, laid out to dry, her photograph albums. Tristana, with tears in her eyes, stood observing this picture of desolation, and shot an imploring look at that friend of the family, urging him to leave the poor, sick woman alone. The worst of it was that the good gentleman also had to resign himself to paying the unfortunate family's many expenses, which, what with the endless moving, the frequent breakages and damage to the furniture, mounted relentlessly. That soap-fueled deluge was drowning them all. As luck would have it, after one of those changes of domicile or perhaps because they had arrived in a new house whose walls positively ran with damp or perhaps because Josefina was wearing a pair of shoes that had recently been submitted to her new cleaning system, the time came for her to surrender her soul to God. A rheumatic fever, which rampaged through her body, sword in hand, brought an end to her sad days. The most depressing aspect of her death was that, in order to pay the doctor, the pharmacist, and the undertaker, as well as the bills that Josefina had run up buying food and perfumes, Don Lope had to dig still deeper into his already depleted fortune and sacrifice his most beloved possession: his collection of weapons, ancient and modern, which he had accumulated with all the eagerness and deep pleasure of the connoisseur. The unimaginably noble and austere collection of rare muskets and rusty harquebuses, pistols, halberds, Moorish and Christian flint-locks, hilted swords, breastplates and backplates, which adorned the gentleman's living room along with many other fine objects from the worlds of war and hunting, was sold for a song to a mere hawker. When Don Lope saw his precious arsenal leave his house, he felt troubled and bewildered, but his large soul was nonetheless able to suppress the grief rising up within him and to put on a mask of stoical, dignified serenity. All he had left now was his collection of portraits of beautiful women, which included both delicate miniatures and modern photographs, in which truth replaces art: a museum of his amorous encounters, just as his collection of guns and flags had spoken of the grandeur of a once glorious kingdom. That was all he had left, a few eloquent, albeit silent images, which, while important as trophies, meant very little in terms of base metal.

When she died, Josefina, as so often happens, partly recovered the mind she had lost, and thanks to that, briefly relived her past, recognizing and cursing, like the dying Don Quixote, the follies of her widowhood. Before she turned her eyes to God, she had time to turn them to Don Lope, who was at her side, and to commend to him her orphaned daughter, placing her under his protection; and the noble gentleman accepted this charge effusively, promising what people always promise on these solemn occasions. In short: Reluz's widow closed her eyes, easing, as she passed to a better life, the lives of those who had hitherto been groaning beneath the tyranny of her constant house-moves and cleaning. Tristana went to live with Don Lope and (hard and painful though it is to say), after only two months, he had added her to his very long list of victories over innocence.

4

THE CONSCIENCE of this warrior of love was, as we have seen, capable of shining forth like a bright star, but on other occasions, it revealed itself to be as horribly arid as a dead planet. The problem was that the good gentleman's moral sense lacked a vital component, and like some terribly mutilated organ, it functioned only partially and suffered frequent deplorable breakdowns. In accordance with the fusty old dogma of a knight sedentary, Don Lope accepted neither guilt nor responsibility when it came to anything involving the ladies. While he would never have courted the wife, spouse, or mistress of a close friend, he considered that, otherwise, everything was permitted in matters of love. Men like him, Adam's spoiled brats, had received from heaven a tacit bull that allowed them to dispense with all morality, which was the policeman of the common herd, not the law of the gentleman. His conscience, so sensitive on other points, was, on that point, harder and deader than a pebble, with the difference being that the pebble, when struck by the rim of a wagon wheel, usually gives off a spark, whereas Don Lope's conscience, in affairs of the heart, would have given off no sparks at all even if it had been pounded by the hooves of Santiago's horse.

He professed the most erroneous and tenuous of principles, and backed them up with historical facts, which were as ingenious as they were sacrilegious. He held that in the man-woman relationship, the only law is anarchy—if anarchy can be a law—and that sovereign love should bow only to its own intrinsic rules, and that any external limitations placed on its sovereignty weakened the race and impoverished the blood flowing through humanity's veins. He said, rather wittily, that the articles of the Ten Commandments dealing with the *peccata minuta* had been added by Moses to God's original work for purely political reasons, and that those reasons of State have continued to influence successive ages, necessitating some policy of the passions; however, as civilization has progressed, those reasons have lost all logical force, and the fact that the effects subsisted long after the causes had disappeared was due entirely to habit and human idleness. Repeal of those outdated articles was long overdue, and the legislators should stop shilly-shallying and set to work. Society itself was crying out for such changes, rejecting what their leaders insisted on preserving despite growing pressure from the customs and realities of life. Ah, if that good old man Moses were to look up, he would be the first to correct his work, recognizing that life moves on.

Needless to say, all those who knew Garrido, myself included, abominate such ideas and wholeheartedly deplore the fact that this foolish gentleman's conduct proved to be such a faithful application of his perverse doctrines. It should be added that among those of us who value the major principles that form the basis . . . etcetera, etcetera . . . , it makes our hair stand on end just to think what the social machine would be like if its enlightened operators took it into their heads to adopt Don Lope's mad ideas and repeal the articles or commandments which he, in word and deed, proclaimed useless. If hell did not exist, it would be necessary to create one just for Don Lope, so that he could spend an eternity doing penance for his mockery of morality and thus serve as a perennial lesson for the many who, while without openly declaring themselves to be his supporters, are nonetheless to be found throughout this sinful world of ours.

The gentleman was very pleased with his acquisition, for the girl was pretty, bright, with graceful gestures, firm skin, and a seductive voice. "Let them say what they like," he said to himself, remembering the sacrifices he had made in supporting her mother and saving her father from dishonor, "I've earned her. Didn't Josefina ask me to take care of her? Well, what better care could she have? I'm certainly keeping her safe from harm. Now no one would dare to touch so much as the hem of her garment." At first, our gallant took exquisite pains to guard his treasure; he feared she might rebel, startled by the difference in age, far greater than allowed for by the rules of love. He was assailed by fears and doubts; in his conscience he came very close to feeling something like a faint tickling, the precursor of remorse. That did not last long, however, and the gentleman soon recovered his usual robust self-confidence. In the end, the devastating action of time dulled his enthusiasm sufficiently for him to relax the rigor of his restless vigilance and arrive at a stage similar to that reached by many married couples when the vast capital of tenderness has been spent and they must begin to eke out, with prudent economy, the modest income of a quiet and somewhat insipid affection. We should point out that not for a moment did it occur to the gentleman to marry his victim, for he abhorred marriage; he held it to be the most horrific form of slavery dreamed up by the terrestrial powers-that-be to keep poor humanity under their thumb.

Tristana accepted this way of life almost without realizing the gravity of her situation. Her own innocence, while timidly suggesting to her defensive measures she had no idea how to deploy, also blindfolded her, and only time and the systematic continuance of her dishonor allowed her to gauge and appreciate her sorry plight. She was much handicapped by her neglected education, and her downfall came in the form of the tricks and snares laid for her by that rogue Don Lope, who made up for what the years were taking away from him with verbal subtlety and gallant compliments of the highest order, of the kind hardly used anymore, because those who knew how to use them are a dying breed. While her mature suitor could not capture her heart, he was adept at the skillful manipulation of her imagination, arousing in her a state of false passion, which, to his mind, occasionally resembled the real thing.

Señorita Reluz went through that stormy test like someone suffering the ups and downs of an intense fever, and during it, she experienced moments of brief, pale happiness, tiny hints of what the pleasures of love might be. Don Lope carefully captivated her imagination, sowing it with ideas that encouraged her to accept such a life; he fostered the young woman's readiness to idealize things, to

see them as they are not or as we would like them to be. Most striking of all, in the early days, was that Tristana gave no thought to the
monstrous fact that her tyrant was almost three times her age. To
put this in the clearest possible terms, we have to say that she was
completely unaware of that gap, doubtless due to his own consummate gifts as a seducer and to the perfidious way in which Nature
helped him in his treacherous enterprises, by keeping him in an almost miraculous state of preservation. So superior were his personal
attractions that it proved very difficult for time to destroy them. The
artifice and the false illusion of love could not last, though. One day,
Don Lope realized that the fascination he exercised over the poor
girl had ended, and when she, for her part, came to her senses, she
was profoundly shocked, a state from which she would take a long
time to recover. She suddenly saw the old man in Don Lope, and his
old man's presumption in contravening the laws of Nature by playing the role of the young gallant loomed ever larger in her imagination. Yet Don Lope was not as old as Tristana felt him to be, nor had
he deteriorated to the point where he deserved to be thrown out as a
useless piece of junk, but because, in private, age imposes its own
laws, and it is not so easy to disguise as when one is out and about, in
chosen places and at chosen times, a thousand motives for disillu-
sion arose in her, against which the aging suitor, for all his art and
talent, was defenseless.

Tristana's awakening was merely one stage in the profound crisis
she went through approximately eight months after first losing her
honor, when she was nearly twenty-two. Up until then, Señorita Reluz, who was behind in her moral development, had been all
thoughtlessness and doll-like passivity, with no ideas of her own, living entirely under the influence of someone else's ideas, and so docile
in her feelings that it was easy to evoke them in whatever form and
for whatever purpose one wished. Then there came a time when, like
the shoot of a perennial plant that pushes its way up into life on a
warm spring day, her mind suddenly flowered and filled with ideas,
in tight little buds to begin with, then in splendid clusters. Indeci-
pherable desires awoke in her heart. She felt restless, ambitious, al-

though for quite what she didn't know, for something very far off, very high up, which her eyes could not see; she was occasionally troubled by fears and anxieties, sometimes by a cheerful confidence; she saw her situation with absolute clarity, as well as her own sad lot in humanity; she felt something that had slipped unexpectedly through the doors of her soul: pride, an awareness that she was no ordinary person; she was surprised by the growing hubbub in her intellect, saying: "Here I am. Haven't you noticed the grand thoughts I have?" And as the doll's stuffing was gradually changing into the blood and marrow of a woman, she began to find the mean little life she led in the grip of Don Lope Garrido both boring and repugnant.

5

AND AMONG the thousand and one things Tristana learned during that time, without anyone having to teach her, was the art of dissembling, making use of the ductility of words, adding flexible springs to the mechanism of life, dampers to muffle the noise, the kind of skillful deviations from the rectilinear path that are almost always dangerous. For, without either of them realizing it, Don Lope had made her his pupil, and some of the ideas that were now blooming afresh in her young mind sprang from the seedbed of her lover's and, alas for her, her teacher's mind. Tristana was at the age and season of life when ideas stick, when the most serious contagions of personal vocabulary, manners, and even character occur.

The young lady and the maid became close friends. Without the company and care of Saturna, Tristana's life would have been intolerable. They chatted while they worked and, when they rested, chatted some more. Saturna told her about her life, painting a genuinely realistic picture of the world and of men, neither blackening nor poeticizing either; and Tristana, who barely had a past life to recount, threw herself into the empty spaces of supposition and presumption, building castles for her future life, the way children do out of a few bricks and some earth. History and poetry came together in happy marriage. Saturna taught and Don Lope's little girl created, basing her bold ideals on the other woman's deeds.

"Look," Tristana would say to Saturna, who was more true friend than servant, "not everything that perverse man teaches us is nonsense, and there's more to some of what he says than meets the eye. Because you can't deny he has talent. For example, what he says about matrimony is absolutely right, don't you think? For my part—and I know you'll tell me off for this—I think the whole idea of chaining yourself to another person for the rest of your life is the invention of the devil. Don't you agree? You'll laugh when I tell you that I never intend to marry, that I'd like to remain forever free. I know what you're thinking, that I'm worrying needlessly, because after what this man has done to me and having no money of my own, no one's going to want to take me anyway. Isn't that right?"

"No, Señorita, I wasn't thinking that at all," Saturna replied at once. "There's a pair of trousers for every occasion, and that includes marriage. I was married once myself, and while I don't regret it one bit, I certainly wouldn't bother going to the altar again. Yes, freedom, Señorita, that's the word, although it isn't one that sounds good in a woman's mouth. You know what they call women who kick over the traces, don't you? They call them free—free and easy. So if you want to preserve your reputation, you have to submit to a little slavery. If women had trades and careers, as all those rascally men do, that would be another matter. But there are only three careers open to those who wear skirts: marriage, which is a career of sorts; the theater...working as an actress, which isn't a bad way of earning your living; and...well, I'd rather not mention the third one. I'll leave that to your imagination."

"Well, given the choice, I don't much like the first, still less the third, but I would certainly take up the second if I had any talent, except I really don't think I have. I know it's hard to be free—and honest. And what does a woman with no income live on? If they'd let us be doctors, lawyers, even pharmacists, or scribes, if not government ministers or senators, then we would be able to manage, but sewing? How many stitches would you have to sew in order to maintain a household? When I think what will become of me, I feel like crying. If I could be a nun, I'd be applying for a place right now, but I couldn't stand being shut up for the rest of my life. I want to live, to see the world and find out why we're here. Yes, I want to live and be free. Do you think a woman could become a painter and earn money painting pretty pictures? Paintings are expensive. My father paid a thousand pesetas for one that was nothing but a few mountains in the background, four bare trees, and in the foreground a pond with two ducks on it. Or could a woman perhaps become a writer and write plays or prayer books or even fables? That seems easy enough to me. These last few nights, lying awake and not knowing how to fill the time, I've invented all kinds of dramas, some that would make you cry and others that would make you laugh, and stories with complicated plots and bursting with tremendous passions, and I don't know what else. The trouble is I can't write, I mean, not neatly, and I make all kinds of grammatical errors and even spelling mistakes. But ideas, if they are ideas, I've no shortage of them."

"Ah, Señorita," said Saturna, smiling and raising her fine dark eyes from the stocking she was darning, "you are much deceived if you think that something like that would be enough to feed a free and honest lady! That's for men to do, and even then…the ones who live solely on their imaginations never get fat. They may use feather quills, but when it comes to feathering their own nests, they don't stand a chance. For example, Pepe Ruiz, my late husband's foster brother, who knows about these things because he works in the foundry where they make the lead letters for printing presses, he always used to say that it's nothing but hunger and poverty for people who live by the pen, and that in Spain you don't earn your daily bread by the sweat of your brow but with your tongue, meaning that the only ones who get rich are the politicians who spend their lives speechifying. Brain work? Forget it! Dramas and stories and books that make you laugh and cry? Mere talk. The people who write those things won't earn enough to feed themselves unless they've got friends in high places. That's how things work in gov'ment."

"Well, do you know what I think?" said Tristana with great feeling. "I think I could make a go of it in government or politics too. No, don't laugh. I know how to make speeches. It's really easy. I would just have to read a few reports of the debates in parliament and I could cobble together enough words to fill half a newspaper."

"No, you have to be a man to do that, Señorita! Our petticoats get in the way, just like they do when it comes to riding a horse. My late husband always used to say that if he hadn't been so shy, he would have gone farther than most, because he used to come up with the kind of bright ideas you hear in parliament, from a Castelar or a Cánovas, you know, ways of saving the country and all that; but whenever the poor old thing wanted to say his piece at the Working Men's Circle or at meetings with his 'colleagues,' his throat would tighten and he couldn't even get the first word out, and that's always the most difficult part, he just couldn't get started. And of course if he couldn't get started, he couldn't be an orator or a politician."

"Oh, how stupid. I certainly wouldn't have any trouble getting started," Tristana said, then added in a discouraged tone, "The problem is we're stuck, tied down in a thousand ways. I've also thought that I could perhaps learn other languages. I've only got a smattering of French, which I learned at school, and I'm already forgetting that. But how wonderful to be able to speak English, German, Italian! It seems to me that I could, that I'd be a quick learner too. I have a sense—how can I put it?—I have a sense that I already know a little before I've even started studying, as if I had been English or German in another life and that had left a kind of linguistic trace in me."

"Now languages," said Saturna, looking at Tristana with maternal solicitude, "that's something that would be worth learning, because you can earn quite a lot from teaching, and, besides, it would be good to be able to understand what foreigners were going on about. Perhaps the master could find you a good teacher."

"Don't mention your master to me. I expect nothing from him." Then thoughtfully, staring at the light, she said, "I don't know when or how this will end, but it will have to end somehow."

She fell silent, plunged in somber thought. Pursued by the idea of escaping Don Lope's house, she could hear in her mind the deep rumble of Madrid, she could see the dusting of lights shining in the distance, and she felt entranced by the idea of independence. Emerging from her meditations as if from a lethargy, she gave a long sigh. How lonely she would be in the world away from the house of her poor, aged gallant! She had no relatives, and the only two people she could call "relatives" were far, far away: her maternal uncle, Don

Fernando, was in the Philippines, and her cousin Cuesta was in Majorca, and neither of them had ever shown the slightest desire to help her. She recalled too (while Saturna watched with sympathetic eyes) that the families who had been friends of her mother's and used to visit them regularly, now regarded her coolly and with suspicion, the effect of the diabolical shadow cast by Don Lope. In response, Tristana took refuge in her pride, and despising those who insulted her gave her the kind of ardent feeling of satisfaction which, like alcohol, briefly fills one with courage, but in the long run destroys.

"Come on now, enough of these gloomy thoughts!" said Saturna, flapping her hand in front of her eyes, as if shooing away a fly.

6

"WHAT do you expect me to think about? Happy things? Well, where are they?"

To lighten the mood, Saturna would change the subject to something jollier, regaling Tristana with anecdotes and gossip from the garrulous society around them. On some nights, they would amuse themselves by making fun of Don Lope, who, finding himself in such straitened circumstances, had rejected the splendid habits of a lifetime and become rather stingy. Squeezed by his growing penury, he had cut back on the already minimal household expenses and was educating himself—at last!—in the art of domestic economics, so at odds with his chivalric philosophy. Grown meticulous and fussy, he now intervened in matters he had once deemed incompatible with his lordly decorum, and his new scowling, curmudgeonly demeanor disfigured him far more than the deep lines on his face and his graying hair. The two women drew much amusement and diversion from the misfortunes and the belatedly banal preoccupations of this fallen Don Juan. The comical thing was that since Don Lope knew absolutely nothing about the economics of the home, the more he prided himself on being a financier and a good administrator, the more easily Saturna found it to deceive him, being a past mistress in the art of pilfering and in the other skills required of cooks and those who go to market.

With Tristana, he was always as generous as his ever-worsening financial circumstances would allow. The beginnings of their growing poverty were quite sad enough, but it was in the area of clothes that a painful reduction in expenditure made itself most keenly felt.

Don Lope, however, sacrificed his own vanity to that of his slave, which was no small sacrifice for a man who was such a devoted admirer of himself. Then came the day when poverty revealed its bare skull in all its ugliness, and both Don Lope and Tristana found themselves wearing equally threadbare, antiquated outfits. Aided by Saturna, the poor girl would sit up late at night laboring over her few poor rags, finding a thousand ways to recast them, each one a marvel of skill and patience. In the brief period we might describe as happy or golden, Garrido occasionally used to take her to the theater, but necessity, with its heretic's face, decreed, at last, the absolute suppression of all public spectacles. Her horizons closed in and grew ever darker, and that poor, disagreeable household, empty of all emotional warmth and devoid of any pleasing occupations, weighed heavy on her spirit. For the house, which still contained the remnants of certain luxurious furnishings, was becoming unimaginably ugly and sad; every object spoke of penury and decay; nothing that was broken or run down was mended or repaired. In the icy, plundered living room, among various hideous items of furniture, stood an ornate *bargueño* desk that had been much battered in various removals, and in which Don Lope kept the record of his love life. On the walls were the nails on which his displays of weapons had once hung. His study was crammed with things that cried out for more space, and in the dining room all that remained was the table and some rickety chairs whose leather upholstery was all dirty and torn. The sheer monumental bulk of Don Lope's wooden bed, complete with columns and an elegant canopy, still impressed, but the blue damask curtains hung in tatters. Tristana's room, next to her master's, was the least marked by disaster, thanks to the exquisite care with which she defended the furnishings from disintegration and poverty.

And while the house declared, in the expressive way things do, the unstoppable decline of that knight sedentary, the gallant himself was rapidly becoming a painful image of the vain and fleeting nature of human glory. Dejection and sadness at his own ruination must have had much to do with the "fall" of that needy gentleman, deepening the lines on his forehead far more than the years or the rumbustious life he had led since he was in his twenties. His hair, which had started to gray when he was forty or so, had always remained strong and thick; now, however, it was beginning to fall out in clumps, which he would have restored to their rightful place had there been some appropriate alchemy available. His teeth were in good condition, at least those that were visible; but his hitherto admirable molars were beginning to rebel, refusing to chew his food properly or else breaking off, as if they were biting into each other. His soldierly features were gradually losing their firm lines, and it took an iron will to preserve his hitherto slender figure. At home, his will slackened, reserving its efforts for the street, for walks, and for the club.

Normally, if he found both women still awake when he came back at night, he would pause to chat with them, briefly with Saturna, whom he would then dispatch to bed, and at greater length with Tristana. There came a time, though, when he would nearly always enter silently and irritably and go straight to his room, where the poor captive Tristana would have to listen and put up with his complaints about his persistent cough, his rheumatism, or his difficulty in breathing. Don Lope would curse and swear, as if he believed that Nature had no right to make him suffer or as if he considered himself to be a favored mortal, immune to the miseries afflicting the rest of humanity. To make matters worse, he found himself obliged to sleep with his head wrapped in an ugly cloth, and his bedroom stank of the concoctions he used for his rheumatism and his catarrh.

But these trifles, which cut Don Lope's pride to the quick, did not affect Tristana as much as the annoying obsessions that began to take hold of the poor gentleman, for along with his pitiful physical and moral collapse, he began to be pricked by jealousy. Sensing that he was now an old lion, he, who had never considered any other man his rival, was suddenly filled with anxieties and saw robbers and enemies hiding in his very shadow. Aware of his own decrepitude, he was devoured by egotism, like a kind of senile leprosy, and the idea that the poor young woman should compare him, even if only mentally, with imagined exemplars of youth and beauty, soured his life. His good judgment, it should be said, did not desert him entirely, and in his lucid moments, which usually occurred in the morning, he recognized the inappropriateness and irrationality of his behavior and tried to calm his captive with trusting, affectionate words.

These moments of calm did not last long, however, because when night fell, and the old man and the girl were alone, the former sank back into his atavistic egotism, submitting her to humiliating interrogations and, once, overwhelmed by the torment he felt at the alarming gap between his morbid frailty and Tristana's vigor and freshness, he went so far as to say, "If I ever find out you've been deceiving me, I'll kill you, believe me, I'll kill you. I would prefer to end my life tragically than be a decrepit old cuckold. You had best commend your soul to God before you even think of being unfaithful. Because I know. There are no secrets for me. I possess an infinite knowledge of these things, as well as having a whole lifetime of experience and an infallible nose...you can't fool me."

7

TRISTANA felt vaguely frightened, but not terrified, nor did she quite believe her master's fierce threats, sensing that his boasts about his infallible nose and his powers of divination were a trap he laid to control her. Her easy conscience armed her with courage against the tyrant, and she didn't even bother to obey his many prohibitions. He had ordered her not to go out with Saturna, but she escaped almost every afternoon, not to Madrid proper but to Cuatro Caminos, Partidor, Canalillo, or toward the hills above the Hippodrome; a walk in the country, usually with a picnic, moments of healthy relaxation. These were the only times in her life when the poor slave could set aside her sadness and enjoy herself with childlike abandon, allowing herself to run and jump and play tag with the innkeeper's daughter, who used to go with her, or some other friend from the neighborhood. On Sundays, the walk was of an entirely different nature. Saturna had placed her son in the local hospice and, along with all the other mothers who found themselves in the same situation, she would go and see him when the boys were allowed out.

Usually, when the throng of boys reached an agreed spot among the new streets of Chamberí, the order was given to break ranks and then they were free to play. Waiting for them were their mothers, grandmothers, and aunts (those who had them), who came bearing small bundles containing oranges, peanuts, hazelnuts, cakes, or crusts of bread. Some of the boys would run about playing games with sticks; others joined the groups of women. Some begged coins off passersby, and almost all of them milled around the vendors of barley sugar, hazelnuts, and pine nuts. Tristana always enjoyed watching them, and when the weather was fine, she never missed a chance to share with her servant the pleasant task of spoiling the young boarder, who was called Saturno after his mother, and was stocky and knock-kneed, although his chubby red cheeks were a testament to the healthy diet at the hospice. The rough cloth uniform he wore didn't really allow for elegance of movement, and his braided cap was too small for his large head, which was covered with a stiff brush of hair. His mother and Tristana found him most amusing, but it has to be said that he hadn't an ounce of wit in him; he was, rather, docile, good-hearted, and hardworking, with a taste for mock bullfights. Tristana would always bring him a gift of an orange and a penny so that he could buy himself some sweets; and however much his mother urged him to save, suggesting that he put away the money he was given, she could never check his extravagance, and any coin acquired was a coin immediately put back into circulation. Thus commerce prospered thanks to the paper windmills he bought, as well as the banderillas for his bullfights and bags of toasted chickpeas and acorns.

After a long period of importunate and annoying rain, October brought a tranquil two weeks, with warm sun, clear skies, and windless days; and although Madrid still woke up to mornings shrouded in mist, and the night chill considerably cooled the earth, the afternoons, from two until five, were a delight. On Sundays, not a living soul stayed at home, and every street in Chamberí, the Altos de Maudes, the avenues leading up to the Hippodrome, and the hills of Amaniel were all thronged with people. There was a constant hurrying stream of picnickers heading for Tetuán. On one such glorious October Sunday, Saturna and Tristana went to wait for the boys in Calle de Ríos Rosas, which joins Santa Engracia and Paseo de la Castellana, and on that lovely, broad, straight, sunny road, which looks out over a vast expanse of countryside, two lines of little prisoners were given their freedom. Some clung to their mothers, who had been following at a distance, while others immediately began staging one of their bullfights complete with bare-horned young bulls, a president of the bullring, a bull pen, inner and outer barriers, the separating out of good bulls from bad, as well as music from the hospice and other traditional touches. On that occasion, they were joined by a group of children in blue overcoats and braided caps; they were from the local school for deaf, dumb, and blind children, each deaf-mute child being paired with a blind child. The eyes of the dumb child meant that the blind child could walk without stumbling, and they communicated by means of furious touches and taps, amazing to watch. Thanks to the accuracy of that language, the blind children soon realized that the children from the hospice were there too, while the dumb children, all eyes, longed to take their turn performing a few passes with the "bulls," as if they needed the gift of speech to do so! The system of gestures used among the deaf-mutes was often incredibly subtle and quick, as agile and flexible as the human voice. Their bright faces, their eyes alive with language, were in marked contrast to the bored, dead, horribly pockmarked faces of the blind children, whose eyes were either empty and closed beneath a fringe of rough lashes or open but oblivious to light, their pupils like curdled glass.

They stopped and, for a moment, thanks to endless gestures and grimaces and touches, fraternity between the two groups reigned. Then the blind children, unable to take part in any of the games, moved disconsolately away. Some allowed themselves a smile, as if they could see, their knowledge of what was happening communicated to them through a rapid tapping of fingers. The sight of those poor wretches inspired Tristana with such compassion that it almost hurt her to look at them. Imagine not being able to see! They were not whole people: they lacked the ability to understand, and how wearisome to have to understand everything through the mind alone!

Saturno left his mother's side to join a group of boys who, having posted themselves in a convenient spot, were robbing passersby not of their money but of their matches. "Your matches or your life," was their watchword, and this plundering brought the boys more than enough material for their pyrotechnical experiments or, indeed, for Inquisitorial bonfires. Tristana went to look for him, but before she drew near, she saw a man talking to the deaf-mute children's teacher, and when her eyes met his—because they saw and looked at each at the same moment—she felt an inner shudder, as if her blood had momentarily ceased to flow.

Who was he? She had probably seen him before, but she couldn't remember when or where, whether there or somewhere else; but this was the first time she had felt such profound surprise on seeing him, surprise mingled with confusion, joy, and fear. Turning her back on him, she spoke to Saturno, warning him of the dangers of playing with fire, but she could hear the stranger's voice talking energetically about things she could not understand. When she looked at him again, she felt that he, in turn, was searching her out with his eyes. Embarrassed, she moved off, determined, however, to steal another glance at him from a distance, eager to observe with a woman's eyes this man who, for no apparent reason, so demanded her attention, to see if he was dark or fair, if he wore elegant clothes, if he was some-one of importance, because she had not as yet established any of those things. He, in turn, moved off: He was young, quite tall, and his clothes were those of an elegant person who cannot be bothered to get dressed up; on his head he wore a slightly crumpled beret and, loosely grasped in his right hand, he carried a very worn summer overcoat. He appeared to give little importance to clothes. His suit was gray, his cravat a carelessly tied bow. All this she took in at a glance, and she found this gentleman, or whatever he was, very attractive; he was dark-complexioned and had a short beard . . . For a moment, she wondered if he was wearing glasses, but no, nothing covered his eyes, which were . . . but because he was now some distance away, Tristana couldn't quite tell what his eyes were like.

He vanished, but his image lingered in the mind of Don Lope's slave, and the following day, when she was out walking with Saturna, she saw him again. He was wearing the same suit, but this time he had his coat on and a white scarf around his neck, because there was a cool breeze blowing. She regarded him with a kind of brazen innocence, delighted to see him again, and he returned her gaze, stopping a discreet distance away. "It's as if he wanted to speak to me," she thought. "But why doesn't he just say what he has to say." Saturna was laughing at this timid exchange of glances, and Tristana, blushing, pretended to laugh too. That night, she could not rest and, not daring to reveal her feelings to Saturna, she had these very grave thoughts: "I really like him! I wish he would get up the courage to speak. I don't know who he is and yet I think about him night and day. What *is* going on? Am I mad? Is this just the despair of the prisoner who has discovered a tiny hole through which she can escape? I don't know what all this means, I only know that I need him to speak to me, even if only by signs, like the deaf-mute children, or for him to write to me. It doesn't frighten me the idea of writing to him first or saying 'Yes' before he has even asked me...What madness! But I wonder who he is. He might be a rogue, a...No, he's clearly not like other people. He's the only one, that much is clear. There is no one else. And fancy meeting the 'only one' and finding that he's even more afraid than I am of telling me that I'm his 'only one'! No, I'll speak to him, I'll go over and ask him the time or something, or I'll be like the hospice boys and beg a match off him. What nonsense! What would he think of me? He'd think I was a flibbertigibbet. No, he has to be the one to approach me."

The following evening, when it was almost dark, when mistress and servant were traveling on the open-top tram, there he was again! They saw him get on at the Glorieta de Quevedo, but because the tram was quite crowded, he had to stand on the platform at the front. Tristana felt so breathless that she occasionally had to stand up in order to breathe more easily. She felt a terrible weight pressing on her lungs, and the idea that, when she got off the tram, the stranger might decide to break his silence filled her with confusion and trepidation. What would she say to him? She would have no alternative but to pretend to be shocked, alarmed, and offended, to reject him outright and tell him "No." That would be the polite, decent thing to do. They got off, and the gentleman followed them at a chaste distance. Don Lope's slave didn't dare to look back, but Saturna took it upon herself to do so for them both. They kept stopping for the most obscure reasons, retracing their steps to look in a shopwindow, but the gentleman remained as silent as a Trappist monk. In their disorderly wanderings, the two women bumped into some boys playing on the pavement, and one of them fell to the ground, screaming, while the others raced for their houses, making a devil of a racket. There was general confusion, a childish tumult, angry mothers rushing to their front doors... So many helpful hands reached out to pick up the fallen boy that another fell over too, and the noise only grew.

While all this was going on, Saturna noticed that her mistress and the handsome stranger were standing a matter of inches apart, and so she crept away. "Thank heavens," she thought, spying on them from afar, "he's taken the bait; they're talking at last." What did Tristana say to the young man? We don't know. All we know is that Tristana answered "Yes" to everything, "Yes, Yes, Yes..." getting ever louder, like someone who, overwhelmed by feelings stronger than her own will, loses all sense of propriety. She was like someone drowning, grabbing hold of a piece of wood, believing it will save her, and it would be absurd to expect her to behave in a decorous fashion as she seizes hold of that plank. The brief, categorical responses given by Don Lope's little girl, that "Yes" pronounced three times with growing intensity of tone, was the profound voice of the preservation instinct speaking, a cry for help from a desperate soul. The little scene was brief and profitable.

When Tristana returned to Saturna's side, she put her hand to her brow and, trembling, said, "I must be mad. Only now do I realize how mad. I showed no tact, no guile, no dignity. I surrendered myself, Saturna. Whatever will he think of me? I just didn't know what I was doing... I was simply dragged along by some kind of vertigo... I answered 'Yes' to everything he said... as if, oh, you've no idea, as if my soul were pouring out through my very eyes. *His* eyes were burning into me. And there I was thinking I knew some of those useful female wiles! He'll think I'm an idiot, that I have no shame. But I just couldn't pretend or play the shy little miss. The truth leapt to my lips and my feelings overflowed. I tried to drown them out and ended up drowning. Is that what being in love is? All I know is that

I love him with all my heart, and that's more or less what I said. How shameful! I love him and yet I don't even know him, I don't know who he is or even his name. This isn't how love affairs should start ... not usually anyway, they should develop by stages, with a few sly yeas and nays along the way, with some degree of cunning. But I can't be like that: I surrender my heart when it tells me to surrender it. What do you think, Saturna? Will he think I'm a loose woman? Advise me, guide me. I don't know about these things. Wait, listen: Tomorrow, when you come back from doing the shopping, you'll find him on the corner where we spoke and he'll give you a note for me. By all that's most precious to you, by the health of your own son, Saturna, please don't refuse me this favor, I'll be eternally grateful. Bring me that little piece of paper, I beg you, if you don't want me to die tomorrow."

8

"I've loved you ever since I was born..." Thus began the first letter, no, the second, which was preceded by a brief conversation in the street, huddled under a streetlamp, a conversation that was interrupted with hypocritical severity by Saturna, and during which the lovers spontaneously addressed each other as *tú*, without any prior agreement, as if there were no other possible form of address. She was astonished at how her eyes had deceived her when she had first encountered this stranger. When she had seen him that afternoon with the deaf-mute children, she took him for a grown man of some thirty or more years. How silly! He was a mere boy! He couldn't be more than twenty-five, although he did have a slightly pensive, melancholic air about him, more appropriate to someone older. She knew now that his eyes shone, that his dark skin was tanned by the sun, that his voice was like soft music, of a kind Tristana had never heard before and which, once she had heard it, soothed the very cells of her brain. "I've loved you and been looking for you ever since before I was born," said her third letter, a letter imbued with a kind of wild spiritualism. "Don't think badly of me if I show myself to you with no veil of any kind, because the veil of false decorum with which the world orders us to disguise our feelings crumbled in my hands when I tried to put it on. Love me as I am, and were I ever to discover that you had interpreted my sincerity as forwardness or shamelessness, I would not hesitate to take my own life."

And he wrote to her: "The day I found you was the last day of a long exile."

And she: "If, one day, you find in me something that displeases you, please be kind enough to conceal your discovery from me. You are a good man and if, for any reason, you were to cease loving me or caring for me, you would deceive me, wouldn't you, allowing me to believe that your feelings for me remained the same? Kill me a thousand times over rather than stop loving me."

And after these things had been written, the world did not fall apart. On the contrary, everything remained the same on earth and in heaven. But who was he, this young man? Horacio Díaz was the son of a Spanish father and an Austrian mother from the country known as *Italia irredenta*; he was born at sea, when his parents were sailing from Fiume to Algeria, and was subsequently brought up in Oran until he was five; in Savannah, Georgia, until he was nine; and in Shanghai until he was twelve—cradled by the ocean waves, transported from one world to another, he was the innocent victim of the wandering and eternally expatriate life of his consul father. After all those comings and goings and wearisome traipsing about the globe and under the influence of those many diabolical climates, his mother died when he was only twelve and his father when he was thirteen, leaving him in the power of his paternal grandfather, with whom he lived in Alicante for fifteen years, suffering more under his fierce despotism than the poor galley slaves forced to row in those heavy, ancient ships.

And now hear the gabbled words that issued forth from Saturna's mouth, more whispered than spoken: "Oh, Señorita, what a palaver! I went to see him, as arranged, at number five in that street down there, and I boldly attacked those wretched stairs. He said he lived on the top floor, the very top, and so I kept on going, up and up, with another flight of stairs always before me. It still makes me smile. It's a new house. Inside, there's a courtyard surrounded by rooms that are rented out by the week, and then floors and more floors, until finally...It's like a dovecote that place, with lightning rods for neighbors and a view of the very clouds themselves. I thought I'd never arrive. Finally, lungs heaving, I got there. Imagine a really big room, a huge window with all the light from the sky flooding in, the walls painted red and hung with paintings, bare canvases, heads without bodies, bodies without heads, pictures of women, breasts and all, hairy men, arms without people and faces without ears, all the very color of our own flesh. Honestly, all that nudity was downright embarrassing. Then there were divans, antique-looking chairs, plaster busts with blank eyes and hands and bare feet... all made of plaster too. A big easel, and another smaller one, and resting on the chairs or nailed to the walls, paintings small and large, some finished, some not, some showing a nice patch of blue sky, as bright as the real one, and then a bit of a tree, some railings, and a few potted plants; and in another there were some oranges and peaches... really beautiful. Anyway, to cut a long story short, there were some pretty fabrics too and a suit of armor like the ones warriors used to wear. Oh, it did make me smile! And there he was with his letter already written. And me being a nosy parker, I asked him if he lived in that rather drafty place, and he said yes and no, because he sleeps at his aunt's house in Monteleón, but spends the day there and has his lunch in one of those cafés next to the water tower."

"I knew he was a painter," said Tristana, barely able to breathe for sheer joy. "What you saw was his studio, silly. Oh, it must be really lovely!"

As well as furiously writing to each other every day, they met each afternoon. Tristana would leave the house with Saturna, and Horacio would be waiting for them just this side of Cuatro Caminos. Saturna would then let them go off on their own, hanging back discreetly so as to allow them all the time they needed to wander along the lush banks of the Oeste or Lozoya canals or the arid slopes of Amaniel. He wore a cloak and she a little veil and a short overcoat, and they would walk along arm in arm, oblivious to the world, its troubles and its vanities, living entirely for each other and for a dual "I," as they strolled dreamily along or sat, enraptured, together. They spoke mainly about the present, but autobiography also somehow slipped into their sweet, confiding conversations, all love and idealism, all billing and cooing, with the occasional fond complaint or request made, mouth to mouth, by the insatiable egotism that demands a promise to love ever more and more, offering, in turn, an endless increase in love, regardless of the limits set by all things human.

As regards biographical details, Horacio was more forthcoming than Don Lope's slave. She would like to have been equally open and sincere, but felt gagged by her fear of certain dark areas in her past. He, on the other hand, burned to tell her about his life, the unhappiest, saddest youth imaginable; now that he was happy, however, he enjoyed rummaging around in the sad depths of his martyrdom. When he lost both his parents, he was taken in by his paternal grandfather, beneath whose tyranny he suffered and groaned from adolescence through to manhood. Youth? He barely knew the meaning of the word. He was ignorant of the innocent pleasures, childish pranks, and frivolous restlessness with which a boy rehearses the actions of the man. There was no wild beast to compare with this grandfather, no prison more horrible than the dirty, stinking hardware store in which Horacio was kept shut up for some fifteen years, with his grandfather obdurately opposing his grandson's innate love of painting and imposing on him instead the hateful shackles of calculus, and filling his mind up, like stoppers to keep his ideas in, with a thousand and one unpleasant chores involving accounts, invoices, and other such devilry; his grandfather had been the equal of the cruelest tyrants of antiquity or of the modern Turkish empire, and was the terror of the whole family. He sent his wife to an early grave and his male children hated him so much that they all emigrated. Two of his daughters allowed themselves to be carried off and the others made bad marriages in order to escape their father's house.

This tiger took poor Horacio in at the age of thirteen and, as a preventative measure, tethered him by the ankles to the legs of the desk so that he wouldn't be able to stray into the shop or abandon the tedious tasks he was obliged to perform. And if he was found idly drawing pictures with his pen, blows would rain down on him. The tiger wanted, at all costs, to instill in his grandson a love of commerce, because all that stuff and nonsense about art was, in his opinion, nothing but a very stupid way to die of hunger. Horacio's companion in these travails and sufferings was his grandfather's assistant, old and bald as a coot, thin and sallow-complexioned, who, in secret, for fear of riling his master—whom he served as faithfully as a dog—offered the lad his affectionate protection, covering up for any shortcomings and seeking pretexts to take him with him on errands, so that the boy could at least stretch his legs and enjoy a little diversion. The boy was docile and had few defenses against his grandfather's despotism. He preferred to suffer rather than risk angering his tyrant, whose ire was aroused by the slightest thing. Horacio submitted, and soon no longer needed to be tied to the desk and could move with a certain freedom around that foul, stinking den, so dark that the gaslight had to be lit at four o'clock in the afternoon. He gradually adapted to that hideous mold, renouncing childhood, becoming old at fifteen, and unconsciously imitating the long-suffering attitude and the mechanical gestures of Hermógenes, the bald, yellow-skinned assistant, who, having no personality, likewise had no age, and was neither young nor old.

Even though that horrible life shriveled both body and soul, as if they were grapes laid out in the sun, Horacio nevertheless managed to keep alive his inner fire, his artistic passion, and when his grandfather allowed him a few hours of freedom on a Sunday and treated him like a human being, giving him one *real* to spend as he pleased, what did the boy do? He found paper and pencils and drew whatever he saw. It was a terrible torment to him that, although the shop was full of tubes of paint, brushes, palettes, and all the other materials required for the art he so loved, he wasn't allowed to use them. He was always hoping for better times, watching the monotonous days go by, each day the same as the next, like the identical grains of sand in an hourglass. What sustained him was his faith in his destiny, which allowed him to withstand that mean, wretched existence.

His cruel grandfather was as tightfisted as the miserly schoolteacher Cabra in Quevedo's *The Swindler*, and he gave his grandson and Hermógenes just enough food to keep them from starving, with no culinary refinements, as these, in his view, merely clogged up the digestive system. He wouldn't let Horacio play with other boys, because company, even if not entirely bad, served only to corrupt: boys nowadays were as riddled with vices as men. And as for women… that particular aspect of life was the one that most worried the tyrant, and if he had ever discovered that his grandson had developed a soft spot for some girl, he would have beaten him to within an inch of his life. In short, he refused to allow the boy a will of his own, because other people's wills were as much of an obstacle to him as were his own physical aches and pains, and seeing a flicker of self-will in another person provoked in him something like a toothache. He wanted Horacio to embrace the same profession as him, to acquire a taste for "merchandise," for scrupulous accounting, commercial rectitude, and the actual running of the shop; he wanted to make a man of him, a wealthy man; he would arrange a suitable marriage for him, that is, provide a mother for the children he was sure to have, build a modest, orderly house for him, and continue to rule over his existence into old age and over the lives of his heirs and successors too. In order to achieve this aim, which Don Felipe Díaz deemed to be as noble a struggle as the struggle to save his soul, the most important thing was to cure Horacio of his foolish, childish desire to represent objects by applying paint to a piece of wood or canvas. What nonsense! Wanting to reproduce Nature, when Nature was right there in front of his eyes! What was the point of that? What is a painting? A lie, like the theater, a dumb show, and however skillfully painted a sky might be, it could never compare with the real thing. According to him, all artists were fools, madmen, falsifiers, whose sole utility was the money they spent in shops buying the tools of their trade. They were, moreover, vile usurpers of the divine gifts, and were insulting God by trying to imitate him, creating the ghosts or shadows of things that only divine action could and should create; indeed, the hottest spot in hell would be reserved for them for committing such a crime. Don Felipe despised actors and poets for the same reasons, just as he prided himself on never having read a line of poetry or seen a play; he also made much of the fact that he had never traveled, be it by train, carriage, or coach, and had never absented himself from his shop except to attend mass or deal with some matter of extreme urgency.

Thus, his one concern was to remint his grandson in his own unyielding image, and when the boy grew up and became a man, the grandfather's desire to stamp on him his own habits and antiquated obsessions only increased. Because, it must be said, he loved him, yes, why deny it? He had grown fond of him, in the outlandish way that typified all his affections and behavior. Meanwhile, apart from Horacio's still intense vocation for painting, his will had grown flabby with lack of use. Latterly, though, behind his grandfather's back, in a shabby room at the top of the house, which his grandfather agreed that he could use, Horacio carried on with his painting; and there is some suggestion that Don Felipe Díaz knew about this but turned a blind eye to it. This was the first time in his life that he had ever shown any weakness, and it was, perhaps, the precursor to far graver events. Some cataclysm was bound to follow, and so it was: One morning, Don Felipe was in his office going over some English invoices for potassium chlorate and zinc sulfate, when his head dropped forward onto the paper and he died without uttering so much as a sigh. He had turned ninety the day before.

9

HORACIO told all this to his young lady, along with other things that will emerge later on, and she listened with delight, confirmed in her belief that the man heaven had sent her was unique among mortals, and that his life was the strangest and most anomalous of young lives; it almost resembled the life of a saint worthy of inclusion in the list of martyrs.

"That happened," Horacio continued, "when I was twenty-eight, when I had the habits of both an old man and a child, for on the one hand, the terrible discipline imposed on me by my grandfather had preserved in me an innocence and ignorance of the world inappropriate to my age, and on the other, I possessed virtues more appropriate to the very ancient; I felt a kind of weariness about things I had scarcely even encountered; I was filled by a weariness and tedium that made others see me as perennially stiff and numb. Anyway, my grandfather left a very large fortune, amassed penny by penny in that vile, malodorous shop. I got a fifth part of it; they gave me a lovely house in Villajoyosa, two other smaller country houses, and a corresponding share in the hardware store, which continues to trade under the name of Nephews of Felipe Díaz. On finding myself suddenly free, it took me a while to recover from the stupor into which my independence had thrown me; I felt so timid that when I tried to take a few steps into the world, I stumbled, yes, I stumbled, like someone who cannot walk because he hasn't used his legs in a long time.

"When that wretched brake on my life was finally released, my artistic vocation saved me and made me a man. I didn't hang around to haggle over the execution of the will, I escaped and rushed straight to Italy, my hope, my dream. I had begun to believe Italy didn't really exist, that such beauty was a lie, a mirage. I arrived and the inevitable happened. I was like a seminarian with no vocation who is unleashed upon the world after fifteen years of enforced virtue. You'll understand, I'm sure, how that sudden contact with life awoke in me a wild desire to make up for what I had missed, to live in a matter of months the years that time owed me, having cruelly stolen them from me with the connivance of that fanatical old man. You don't understand? Well, in Venice, I gave myself over to a life of dissipation, going far beyond my own natural instincts, because the old man-child I had become was not nearly as dissolute as he was trying to appear to be, in order to get his own back, to avenge himself on his dull, foolish past self. I came to believe that I was not a real man unless I took licentiousness to extremes, and I amused myself by looking at my reflection in that mirror, a much-begrimed mirror if you like, but one in which I seemed far more elegant than I ever had in my grandfather's back room. Needless to say, I soon grew bored. In Florence and Rome, art cured me of those diabolical desires and, having passed the test, I was no longer tormented by the idea of 'becoming a real man' and began to devote myself to my studies; I launched enthusiastically into drawing from nature; however, the more I learned, the more I became aware of the deficiencies in my artistic education. As regards color, I was fine. I had a natural talent for that, but when it came to drawing, I seemed to grow clumsier with each passing day. How I suffered! How many sleepless nights I spent, how I labored day and night, trying to achieve the right line, struggling with it and giving up, only to return at once to that terrifying battle with renewed energy and fury!

"It *was* infuriating, but how could it be otherwise? Since I hadn't practiced drawing as a child, I had the devil's own job to handle shapes fluently. In my days of slavery, writing endless numbers in Don Felipe's office, I used to amuse myself by giving them human form. I would give the sevens a rather bullying air, as if I were drawing a brief sketch of a man; I made my eights look like buxom women and so on ... and my threes had my grandfather's profile, like the side view of a tortoise. Such childish pursuits were not enough though. They didn't train me to study the lines of objects and reproduce them. I worked, I sweated, I cursed ... and, in the end, I actually did begin to improve. I spent a year in Rome, devoting myself body and soul to formal study, and although I still went out on the occasional drunken spree, as I had in Venice, they were far less boisterous affairs, and I was no longer the overgrown child who, having arrived late at life's party, belatedly gobbles down the dishes already served in order to catch up with those who began eating at the appointed hour.

"I returned to Alicante, where my uncles and aunts had meanwhile divided up my grandfather's legacy, assigning me whatever part they wished, and I never objected or bargained, but said my final farewell to the hardware shop—now transformed and modernized—and came to Madrid, where I have an aunt whom I really don't deserve, an absolute angel, a widow with no children of her own, but who loves and cares for me and spoils me as if I were her own son. She too was a victim of the family tyrant. He used to give her a peseta a day and tell her, in all his letters, that she must save ... As soon as I arrived in Madrid, I dedicated myself entirely to my work. I'm ambitious, I want applause and glory and renown. It saddens me to be a mere zero, worth nothing more than any of the other grains of sand that form the multitude. And until someone convinces me otherwise, I will believe that I contain a fragment, however tiny, of the divine essence that God scattered willy-nilly over the heap.

"I'll tell you something else. Months before I met you, I was plunged into the most dreadful melancholy here in Madrid. There I was with thirty wasted years behind me, and although I knew a little of life and the joys of youth, and could savor, too, certain aesthetic pleasures, I had not known love, had never experienced that sense of fusing my life with that of another person. I began studying abstruse philosophies and, in the solitude of my studio, I struggled with the human form. I had a feeling that love existed only in the desire to obtain it. I fell again into the bitter depressions I had suffered as an adolescent; in my dreams I saw silhouettes, temptingly vague beckoning shapes, whispering lips. I understood then the most subtle of ideas; the most obscure of psychologies seemed to me as clear as the four rules of arithmetic. Then I saw you; you came to meet me. I asked if you were the one and heaven knows what other nonsense. I was so bewildered that you must have thought me utterly ridiculous. However, God decided that you would prove capable of seeing the serious man behind the fool. Our romanticism, our exaltation, struck neither of us as absurd. We came to each other full of hunger, the noble, pure, spiritual hunger that moves the world, which is the reason we exist and will be for the thousands of generations who come after us. I knew you were mine and you declared that I was yours. That is what life is for; what does anything else matter?"

He spoke, and Tristana did not know how to respond, made giddy by such spirituality, as if her lover were hurling clouds of incense at her from a vast thurible. Inside her, emotion was kicking and stamping, like a living being far larger than the breast containing it, and she vented this emotion by laughing wildly or bursting into sudden, passionate tears. It was impossible to say if this feeling was a source of joy to them or a lacerating sorrow, because they both felt as if they had been wounded by a sting that plunged deep into their souls, and were both tormented by a desire for something beyond themselves. Tristana, in particular, was insatiable in her continuous demands for love. She would suddenly utter a bitter complaint that Horacio did not love her enough, that he should love her more, far more; and he would effortlessly provide her with that more-always-more, while demanding the same in return.

At sunset, they contemplated the vast horizon of the Sierra, a vivid turquoise blue with, here and there, different highlights and transparencies, as if that purest of blues had been poured over ice crystals. The curves of the bare hills, appearing and disappearing as if imitating the gentle movement of waves, repeated back to them that "more-always-more," the inextinguishable longing of their hungry hearts. On some afternoons, strolling beside the Canal del

Oeste—an undulating ribbon that winds, like an oasis, around the arid contours of the Madrid landscape—they savored the bucolic peace of that miniature valley. Cocks crowing, dogs barking, little laborers' huts; fallen leaves that the gentle breeze swept into heaps around the trunks of the trees; the donkey grazing calmly and gravely; the slight trembling in the highest branches, which were gradually growing bare; all this aroused in them feelings of delight and amazement, and they spoke to each other of their impressions, in a back-and-forth exchange as if it were simply one impression flowing from lips to lips and springing from eye to eye.

They always returned at the same hour, so that she would not be scolded for staying out late; paying no heed to Saturna, who waited patiently for them, they would walk arm in arm along the Aceiteros path, which, as night fell, became more silent and solitary than the Carretera Mala de Francia. In the west, they saw the sky in flames, the splendid afterglow of the setting sun. Silhouetted against that backdrop, like sharp, black crenellations, stood the cypresses in the cemetery of San Ildefonso, interspersed with sad Grecian-style porticos which, in the half-light, seemed more elegant than they really were. There were few houses and, at that hour, few if any people. They nearly always saw one or two unyoked oxen, of the sort who seem as large as elephants, beautiful creatures bred in Ávila, usually black, with horns that strike fear into the heart of even the bravest of men; beasts made inoffensive by sheer tiredness and who, once the yoke has been removed, want only to lie down and rest and thus regard any passersby with scornful indifference. Tristana would go over to them and place her hands on their curved horns, wishing she had something to feed them.

"Ever since loving you," she would tell her friend, "I haven't felt afraid of anything, not of oxen nor of thieves. I feel almost heroically brave, and wouldn't even flinch if confronted by the horned serpent or the lion."

As they drew near the water tower, they saw, plunged in lonely gloom, the massive bulk of the carousel, where the wooden horses stood poised with their galloping legs outstretched as if bewitched.

The strange shapes of the seesaws and the roller coaster loomed out of the darkness. Since there was no one else about, Tristana and Horacio would briefly monopolize those large toys intended for children, for they, too, were children. Not that far away, they could see the outline of the old water tower, surrounded by dense trees and, over toward the street, the lights of the tram or the passing carriages or some open-air café from which emanated the argumentative voices of a few lingering customers. There among that humble architecture, surrounded by rickety benches and rustic tables, Saturna would be waiting for them, and there they parted, sometimes as sadly and tragically as if Horacio were setting off to the ends of the earth or Tristana were bidding a last farewell before entering a convent. Finally, finally, after many attempts, they managed to part and go their separate ways, still looking back, still just able to make each other out in the gloom of night.

10

NOW THAT she was in love, Tristana, to use her own words, feared neither the hefty oxen or the horned serpent or the fierce Atlas lion, but she was afraid of Don Lope, seeing him as a monster so large that he made all the wild, dangerous beasts of creation seem small. Analyzing her fear, though, she judged it to be such that it could, at any given moment, change into blind, bold valor. The differences between captive and tyrant grew more marked by the day. Don Lope reached new heights of impertinence and although, in agreement with Saturna, Tristana concealed from him her evening sorties, when the old gallant said to her, grim-faced, "You're going out, Tristana, I know you are, I can see it on your face," she at first denied it, but then acknowledged it with her disdainful silence. One day, she dared to answer back, "What if I am going out, what of it? Am I to remain shut up in the house for the rest of my life?"

Don Lope gave vent to his rage with threats and curses, and then, half angry, half mocking, said, "Because if you do go out, I can just imagine you being pestered by some good-for-nothing, some carrier of the *Bacillus virgula* of love, the sole fruit of this feeble generation, and the nonsense he might spout could quite simply turn your head. I wouldn't forgive you, my girl. If you're going to be unfaithful to me, at least let it be with a man worthy of me. But then where would you find such a worthy rival? Nowhere! Such a man has not yet been born, nor will be. Indeed, even you must admit that I am not so easily supplanted. Oh, come here, enough of your airs and graces. Do you really think that I don't love you any more? How I would miss you were you to leave me! Out there, you'll find only men of quite staggering insipidness. Come, let us make our peace. Forgive me if I doubted you. You would never deceive me. You're a superior woman, who appreciates the value of people and . . ."

Whatever words Don Lope uttered, whether placatory or angry, they only succeeded in arousing in his captive a deep, unspoken hatred, that sometimes disguised itself as scorn and, at others, as repugnance. She found his company so horribly tedious that she would count the minutes until she could leave and go out into the street. She was terrified that he might fall ill, because then she would not be able to go out. Good God, and what would become of her if she were thus imprisoned, if she couldn't . . . ? No, that was impossible. She would have her evening walk even if Don Lope fell ill or died. At night, Tristana nearly always feigned a headache so that she could escape early from the sight and the odious caresses of that now decrepit Don Juan.

When alone with her passion and her conscience, she would say to herself, "The strange thing is that if this man were to understand that I cannot love him, if he were to erase the word 'love' from our relationship and we could relate to each other in a different way, then I could love him, yes, I could, although I'm not sure how, perhaps as one loves a good friend, because he isn't a bad man, apart from his perverse, monomaniac obsession with pursuing women. I would even forgive him for the wrong he has done me, for my dishonor, I would forgive him with all my heart, as long as he would leave me in peace. Dear God, please make him leave me in peace, and I will forgive him and even feel affection for him, and I will become one of those daughters who is humble to the point of servitude, or like one of those loyal servants who sees a father in the master who feeds them."

Fortunately for Tristana, not only did Don Lope's health improve, thus dispelling her fear that she would have to spend her evenings at home, but he had clearly been offered some relief from his pecuniary difficulties, because his sullen mood lifted, and he regained his usual calm demeanor. Saturna, who was an old dog and a cunning one, told her mistress her thoughts on the matter.

"He's obviously in funds again, because it no longer occurs to him that I should be prepared to work my fingers to the bone for half an endive, nor does he forget the respect he owes, as a gentleman, to those of us who wear a skirt, however darned and patched. The trouble is that when he collects the rent arrears, he spends it all in a week, and then it's farewell chivalry and he's back to his usual rude, fusspot, interfering self."

At the same time, Don Lope once again began to lavish meticulous, almost aristocratic care upon his own person, dressing as carefully as he used to in better days. Both women gave thanks to God for this happy restoration of habits, and taking advantage of the tyrant's regular absences, Tristana flung herself into the ineffable pleasure of going for walks with the man she loved.

In order to provide a change of scene and setting, he would bring a carriage most afternoons, and the two of them would set off to savor the enormous delights of driving so far out of Madrid that they could barely see it. Witnesses to their happiness were the hill at Chamartín, the two pagoda-like towers of the Jesuit college, and the mysterious pine forest; one day, they would follow the road to Fuencarral, the next they would explore the somber depths of El Pardo, where the ground was covered in prickly, metallic-looking leaves, the ash groves that border the Manzanares River, the bare peaks of Amaniel, or the deep ravines of Abroñigal. They would then leave the carriage and go for long walks along the edges of plowed fields, breathing in, along with the fresh air, the pleasures of solitude and stillness, enjoying all that they saw—for all seemed to them lovely, fresh, and new—not realizing that the charm of everything was a projection of their own selves. Turning their gaze on the source of such beauty, namely themselves, they would indulge in the innocent game of pondering their love, a game that, to those not in love, would have seemed cloying in the extreme. They would analyze the reasons for that love, try to explain the inexplicable, decipher the profound mystery of it all, only to end up as they always did: demanding and promising more love, defying eternity, giving guarantees of unalterable fidelity in successive lives lived out in the nebulous circles of that home of perfection, immortality, where souls shake off the dust of the worlds in which they suffered.

Dragging himself back to the more immediate and the more positive, Horacio urged her to come up to his studio, assuring her of the comfort and privacy it offered as a place for them to spend their evenings together. How she longed to see that studio! However, her desire to do so was as strong as her fear that she would become all too fond of that cozy nest and feel so at ease there that she would be unable to leave it. She could guess what might happen in her idol's abode, which, as Saturna put it, had lightning rods for neighbors, or, rather, she did not need to guess, she could see the consequences as clear as day. And she was assailed by the bitter fear that he might then love her less, rather as one loses interest in a hieroglyph once it has been deciphered; she feared, too, that the wealth of her affections might be diminished if she were to take them to the highest level.

Now that love had illuminated her intelligence with new light, filling her mind with ideas and endowing her with the necessary subtlety of expression to be able to translate into words the deepest mysteries of her soul, she was able to explain her fears to her lover with such delicacy and such exquisite turns of phrase that she could express everything she felt without once offending against modesty. He understood, and since they were at one in all things, he responded with similarly tender, spiritual feelings. He did not, however, give up on his wish to take her to his studio.

"And what if we regret it afterwards?" she asked. "Happiness makes me afraid, because when I feel happy, I can feel evil watching me. Instead of draining our happiness to the dregs, what we need now is some difficulty, some tiny crumb of misfortune. Love means sacrifice, and we should always be prepared for self-denial and pain. Demand some major sacrifice of me, some painful obligation, and you will see with what delight I rush to fulfill it. Let's suffer a little, let's be good."

"No one can outdo us when it comes to goodness," said Horacio, smiling. "We are already purer than the angels, my love. And as for imposing suffering on ourselves, there's no need, life will bring us quite enough of that without having to go looking for it. I, too, am a pessimist, which is why when I see goodness standing at the door, I usher it in and refuse to let it leave, just in case the rascal refuses to come back when I need him."

These ideas fired both of them with ardent enthusiasm; words were succeeded by caresses, until a sudden burst of dignity and common sense made them both curb their impatience and clothe themselves once more in formality—an illusion, you might say, but one that saved them for the moment. They talked of serious moral matters; they praised the advantages of virtue and said how beautiful it was to love each other with such exquisite, celestial purity. How much finer and more subtle such a love was and how much more deeply it engraved itself upon the soul. These sweet deceptions bought them time and fed their passion, now with desires, now with the torments of Tantalus, exalting their passion with the very thing that seemed intended to contain it, humanizing it with what should have rendered it divine, so that the bed along which that torrent flowed widened the banks, both spiritual and material.

I I

LITTLE by little, more difficult confessions made their appearance, opening those biographical pages that most resist being opened because they affect one's conscience and one's pride. Asking questions and revealing secrets is all part of love. Confession springs from love, and for that reason twinges of conscience are all the more painful. Tristana wanted to tell Horacio the sad facts of her life and felt that she could not be happy until she did. He glimpsed or, rather, sensed some grave mystery in his beloved's life, and if, at the beginning, out of refinement and delicacy, he preferred not to probe too deeply, the day came when the fears of the man and the curiosity of the lover proved stronger than all his fine intentions. When he met Tristana, he assumed, as did other people in Chamberí, that she was Don Lope's daughter. However, when Saturna took him the second letter, she told him, "She's married, and Don Lope, who you think is her father, is, in fact, her husband."

The young artist was astonished, but not to the extent that he did not believe it. And so it remained and for some days, Horacio continued to see in Tristana, his conquest, the legitimate wife of that elegant, respectable gentleman, who so resembled one of the figures in Velázquez's *Surrender of Breda*. Whenever he mentioned him in her company, he would say, "Your husband this and your husband that ..." and she did not immediately disabuse him. But one day, at last, word by word, question upon question, such was her invincible repugnance for the lie, that Tristana finally found the strength to face up to it and, overwhelmed by shame and sorrow, she set the record straight.

"I've been deceiving you, which I shouldn't and don't want to do. The truth burns to be spoken and I can keep it back no longer. I am not married to my husband, I mean, my papa, I mean to that man . . . I kept meaning to tell you, but I just couldn't. I wasn't sure, I'm still not sure, whether you would feel angry or glad, if I would be worth more or less in your eyes. I've been dishonored, but I'm still a free woman. Which would you prefer me to be: an unfaithful married woman or a spinster who has lost her honor? Even telling you this fills me with shame . . . I don't know . . . I just . . ."

She could not go on and, bursting into bitter tears, pressed her face to her lover's breast. That heartfelt spasm of pain lasted a long time. Neither of them said anything, until, finally, she asked the inevitable question: "Do you love me more or less?"

"I love you as much as I did before, no, more, always more."

It did not take much for her to recount, in broad terms, the how and when of her dishonor. Tears without cease were shed that evening, but in her longing for sincerity, her noble urge to confess, she omitted nothing, as the one sure way of purifying herself.

"He took me in when I was orphaned. He was, it must be said, very generous to my parents. I respected and loved him; I had not the slightest suspicion of what was going to happen. I was too surprised to resist. I was rather more foolish then than I am now, and that wretched man dominated me entirely and dealt with me as he wished. Long before I met you, I hated myself for my weakness of will, and I hate myself all the more now that I know you. Oh, how I have wept! The tears I have shed over my situation! And when I fell in love with you, I felt like killing myself, because I could not offer you what you so deserve . . . What do you think? Do you love me less or more? Tell me that you love me more, always more. In truth, I should seem to you less culpable, since I am not an adulteress; the only person I am deceiving is someone who has no right to tyrannize me. My infidelity, therefore, is not infidelity at all, don't you agree, but a punishment for his infamy; and he thoroughly deserves the wrong I am doing to him."

Horacio could not help but express his jealousy when he learned of the illegitimate nature of the ties that bound Tristana and Don Lope.

"But I don't love him," she said emphatically, "I've never loved him. To tell you the truth, since knowing you, I've begun to feel a terrible aversion for him. And then, oh dear God, I have such strange, mixed feelings. Sometimes it seems to me that I hate him, that I feel for him a loathing as great as the evil he has done to me; sometimes—because I want to be totally frank with you—I feel almost affection, like a daughter, and think that if he treated me as he should, like a father, I would love him . . . Because he isn't a bad man, don't go thinking he's a thoroughly nasty piece of work . . . No, he's a strange mixture of things, a monstrous combination of good qualities and horrible defects; he has two consciences, one very pure and noble in certain respects, the other like a mudhole; and he chooses which to apply depending on the circumstances; he puts them on and off like shirts. He uses his grubby, black conscience for anything to do with love. You see, he was an inveterate womanizer in his time, his conquests too many to count. You can't imagine! Like Don Juan, he left sad memories behind him everywhere, from the aristocracy to the middle classes to the peasantry. He wormed his way into palaces and hovels alike, and the rogue showed no respect for anything, be it virtue, domestic peace, or religion. The wretch has even seduced nuns and other saintly women, indeed, his successes appear to be the work of the Devil. The list of his victims is endless: deceived husbands and fathers; wives who will end up in hell if they aren't there already; children . . . well, one can never be sure who the father is. In short, he is a very dangerous man, because he's a good marksman too and has sent more than a few men into the next world. He cut a very striking figure in his youth and, until only very recently, he could still play a trick or two. Needless to say, his conquests have diminished in number as he's gotten older. I was his last. I belong to his declining years."

Horacio listened to these words indignantly at first and then with amazement, and the only thing it occurred to him to say to his beloved was that she should put an end to that abominable relationship once and for all, but this, the anguished girl replied, was easier said than done, because whenever the wily fellow noticed that she seemed bored or showed a desire to leave, he would immediately play the father figure and become tyrannically affectionate. It would take unusual strength to uproot oneself from such an unpleasant, ignominious life. Horacio urged her to screw up her courage, and the larger the figure of Don Lope loomed in his imagination, the keener became his resolve to deceive the deceiver and snatch from him possibly his last and doubtless his most precious victim.

With her nerves strained to breaking point and feeling poised to commit some rash act, Tristana returned home in a terrible state of moral and mental ferment. She hated her tyrant that night, and when she saw him come in, all smiles and jokes, she felt so enraged that she could happily have thrown her bowl of soup at him. Over supper, Don Lope was witty and talkative, teasing Saturna and saying, among other things, "I know all about your boyfriend in Tetuán, the one they call Juan and a Half because he's so tall, the blacksmith...you know who I mean. Pepe the tram driver told me. That's why you go off wandering each evening, looking for dark corners, often accompanied by a tall, thin shadow."

"I have nothing to do with him, sir. He may well be interested in me, but I have other, far worthier men courting me...even gentlemen. He's not the only fish in the sea."

Saturna was playing along with the joke, while Tristana was burning up inside, and the little she ate tasted like poison. Don Lope had a healthy appetite that night and, like any good bourgeois, steadily munched his way through the chickpea stew, the main course—more mutton than beef—and the grapes that served as dessert, all washed down with the truly awful wine from the local tavern, which the good gentleman drank with true resignation, wincing each time he raised his glass to his lips. Once the meal was over, he withdrew to his room and lit a cigar, summoning Tristana to keep him company. Then, lounging in his armchair, he uttered words that made the young woman tremble.

"Saturna's not the only one enjoying an evening romance. You have your own such romance. Not that anyone has told me as much, but I know you, and for some days now, it's been there to read on your face and hear in your voice."

Tristana turned pale. Her mother-of-pearl complexion took on a bluish tinge in the glow from the lamp lighting the room. She looked like a very beautiful dead girl, and she stood out against the sofa with the dramatic foreshortening of one of those insubstantial Japanese figures, who resemble smiling corpses glued onto the backdrop of a tree or a cloud or some incomprehensible decorative scroll. She finally managed a faint, forced smile, and answered fearfully, "No, you're quite wrong...I don't..."

Don Lope wielded such power over her, such mysterious authority, that in his presence, even though she had ample reasons to rebel, she could not dredge up so much as a breath of willpower.

12

"THERE'S no use denying it," added the decaying Don Juan, taking
off his boots and putting on the slippers that Tristana, to conceal her
state of shock, brought to him from the bedroom next door. "I have
a sharp eye for such things, and the person hasn't yet been born who
can deceive or outwit me. You, Tristana, have found romance, I can
tell from your general state of agitation, from the way you look, from
the dark circles under your eyes, from a thousand other tiny details,
none of which is lost on me. I'm an old dog, and I know that, sooner
or later, any young woman of your age who sallies forth into the
street each day is sure to stumble over a romance of one sort or another. Sometimes good, sometimes ghastly. I don't know what kind
yours is, but for heaven's sake, don't deny that it exists."

Tristana again denied it with gestures and with words, but so un-
convincingly that she would have been far better off keeping quiet.
Don Lope's penetrating gaze frightened and dominated her, filling
her with terror and an amazing inability to lie. Making an enormous effort, she tried not to succumb to the fascination of that gaze
and repeated her denials.

"Deny it if you can," he went on, "but I'm sticking to my guns. I'm
an old tailor and I know my cloth. I'm giving you due warning,
Tristana, so that you may realize your mistake and withdraw before
it's too late, because I really don't like such street romances, although
yours I imagine has, for the moment, gone no further than childish
pranks and innocent games, because if there has been anything
more than that..."

As he said this, he shot poor Tristana such a sharp, menacing look that she recoiled slightly, as if it were not a look but a hand being aimed at her face.

"You be careful, young lady," he said, biting fiercely into his cheap cigar (for he could afford no other kind). "And if you, out of mere flippancy or foolishness, make a laughingstock of me and encourage some good-for-nothing to take me for a . . . No, I'm sure you'll see reason. Because, up until now, no one has ever made a fool out of me. I'm not yet so old that I must put up with such ignominy. Anyway, I will say no more. If it comes to it, I will use my authority to remove you from harm's way and, as a last resort, declare my paternal rights, because, if necessary, I will be obliged to treat you as if I were your real father. Your mother entrusted you to me so that I could protect you, as indeed I have, and I'm determined to save you from all kinds of snares and to defend your honor—"

When she heard this, Tristana could contain herself no longer and, feeling a gust of anger rising in her heart like a hurricane, coming from who knows where, she sprang to her feet and said, "How can you speak of my honor? I have none, because you took it away from me, you ruined me."

She burst into such inconsolable sobbing that Don Lope immediately changed both tone of voice and expression. Putting his cigar down on a pedestal table, he went over to her and clasping her hands, he kissed them and kissed her on the head, too, with genuine tenderness.

"My child, how it wounds me to hear you judge me like that, in such absolute terms . . . The truth is . . . Yes, you're right . . . But you know perfectly well that I don't see you as one of many, as . . . No, not at all. Be lenient with me, Tristana, for you are not a victim; I cannot abandon you, nor will I ever abandon you, and as long as this sad old man you see before you has a crust of bread, it will be yours."

"Hypocrite, fraud, liar!" exclaimed the slave, suddenly aware of her power.

"All right, child, get it off your chest, heap all the insults you want on me," he said, taking up his cigar again, "but allow me to do with you what I have never done with any other woman: to look upon you as someone I love—which is quite a novelty for me—as someone of my own blood. Don't you believe me?"

"No, I don't."

"Well, you'll soon find out. Suffice it to say that I've discovered that you are up to no good. Don't deny it, please. Tell me it's of no significance, a mere bagatelle, a thing of no importance, but don't deny it. Because if I wanted to, I could have you watched . . . but no, spying would be unworthy of you and me. I am merely issuing a warning, to let you know that I can see you, that I know what your game is, that you can hide nothing from me, because, if I wanted to, I could extract the very ideas from your mind and examine them one by one; when you least expect it, I could squeeze out of you even your most hidden thoughts. Be careful, child, and come to your senses. We will speak no more of the matter if you promise me that you will be good and faithful; but if you deceive me, if you exchange my dignity for a handful of soppy words from some dull, snotty-nosed boy, don't be surprised if I defend myself. No one has ever got the better of me yet."

"It's all baseless suspicion on your part," said Tristana, simply in order to say something. "It has never occurred to me—"

"We'll see," said the tyrant, fixing her with another penetrating look. "We've said enough. You are free to come and go as you please, but I warn you, I will not be deceived. I regard you as both wife and daughter, as it suits me. I invoke the memory of your parents—"

"My parents!" exclaimed Tristana, reviving. "If they could rise from their graves and see what you have done to their daughter—"

"God knows that, left alone in the world or in other hands, you would have fared far worse," said Don Lope, defending himself as best he could. "Goodness and perfection do not exist. Let us thank God that he has at least given us the less bad and the relatively good. I don't expect you to venerate me like a saint; I ask only that you see in me the man who loves you with all the many kinds of love that exist, the man who will do anything to save you from evil and—"

"All I see," broke in Tristana, "is gross, monstrous egotism, an egotism that—"

"The tone you take," said Don Lope sourly, "and the energy with which you answer me back only confirm my suspicions, you empty-headed creature. There's some romance here. There's something going on outside the house that makes you loathe what's inside and, at the same time, fills you with ideas of freedom and emancipation. Why not drop the mask? Anyway, I won't let you go. I care about you far too much to surrender you to the perils of the unknown and to dangerous adventures. You're a mere innocent with no knowledge of the world. I may have been a bad father to you, but now I'm going to be a good one."

And adopting the noble, dignified pose that chimed so well with his appearance, and which he used so skillfully when he chose to—putting it on and clanking around in it as if it were a suit of armor—he spoke these grave words: "My child, I will not forbid you to leave the house, because such a prohibition would be unworthy of me and counter to my habits. I do not wish to play the jealous husband or the domestic tyrant, for I know better than anyone how ridiculous they can be. But although I won't forbid you, I will say to you, in all seriousness, that it displeases me greatly to see you go out. You are, to all intents and purposes, free, and any limits on your freedom I leave entirely up to you, always keeping in mind the honor and affection I bear you."

It was a shame he did not speak in verse, for he was the very image of the "noble father" in a Golden Age play! But the effect was rather spoiled by the fact that he spoke in prose and in slippers, which, given his straitened circumstances, were not of the finest quality. That down-at-heel gallant's words nevertheless made an impression on the young woman, who withdrew to the kitchen to weep on the breast of her loyal friend Saturna; however, not half an hour had passed before Don Lope rang the bell to summon her again. She knew by the way in which he rang that it was for her and not Saturna, and she answered the call purely mechanically. No, he did not want any mallow tea or some warm linen, what he wanted was the sweet company of his slave, to fill the sleepless hours of that broken-down libertine, to whom the passing years were like accusing ghosts.

She found him pacing up and down in his room, wearing an old coat over his shoulders, because poverty did not allow him an elegant new dressing gown; his head was bare, as, before she came in, he had removed the cap he usually wore at night. He was a handsome man, to be sure, with the manly, wizened beauty of a figure in a Velázquez painting.

"I called you, my child," he said, sitting down in an armchair and seating his slave on his knees, "because I did not want to go to bed without talking a little more. I won't be able to sleep knowing that you are upset. So tell me about your romance."

"There's nothing to tell," answered Tristana, casually rejecting his caresses, as if distracted.

"Well, I'll find out anyway. I'm not scolding you. You may be misbehaving now, but you've given me much to be grateful for. You loved me in my old age, you gave me your youth, your innocence; I plucked flowers when I was of an age to pick only thistles. I know I acted wrongly and that I should have left you on your stem. But it's too late now; I can't persuade myself that I'm old, because God seems to have placed in my soul a feeling of eternal youth . . . What do you say? What do you think? Do you find it funny? Laugh all you like, but don't leave me. I know I can't gild your prison cell," and he said this with intense bitterness, "because I'm poor. Poverty is another form of old age, although I find it harder to resign myself to the latter than to the former. Being poor weighs on me not for myself but for you, because I would like to surround you with comfort, with the finery you deserve. You should be living like a princess, and here you are living like a poor orphan. I cannot dress you as I would wish to. Fortunately, you look lovely anyway, and in these difficult times, in our always ill-disguised poverty, you are and always will be a pearl."

With gestures rather than with words, he indicated to Tristana that poverty did not bother him in the slightest.

"I know these are things that people say, but rarely feel. We resign ourselves because we have to, but poverty is a very bad thing, my child, something everyone curses. What wounds me most is not being able to gild your little cage. And how beautifully I would gild it too! I could, you know. I was rich once, or, rather, I had money enough to live not just in comfort but in something approaching luxury. You won't remember my bachelor rooms in Calle de Luzón—you were only small then. Josefina brought you there sometimes, and the weapons adorning my living room frightened you. The times I picked you up and carried you around the house, showing you my paintings, my lion and tiger skins, my swords, the portraits of beautiful ladies... and still you were afraid! It was a presentiment perhaps. Who would have thought that a few years later... Even I, who have an infallible instinct where affairs of the heart are concerned, certainly never foresaw this, it never even occurred to me. But what a falling-off there has been since then! I have descended step by step to arrive at this shamefully miserable state. First, I had to get rid of my horses, then my carriage... I left my rooms in Calle de Luzón when they proved too costly. I took different rooms, and then, every few years, had to find something cheaper, ending up in this vulgar, far-flung district. At every stage, at every step, I lost more of the fine, comfortable things with which I had surrounded myself. First, it was my cellar of exquisite wines; then my Flemish and Spanish tapestries, then my paintings, then my beautiful collection of weapons, and all I'm left with now are a few hideous bits of furniture... But I shouldn't really complain, because I still have you, and you are worth more than all the jewels I have lost."

Touched by the noble words of that gentleman in decline, Tristana did not know what to say, because while she did not wish to be evasive, so as not to appear ungrateful, she did not wish to appear too affectionate either, for fear of the consequences. She dare not utter a single tender word that might indicate some weakening of her will, because she knew that the sly fellow would immediately take advantage of the situation. A thought crossed Don Lope's mind, one that he preferred not to express, silenced by the delicacy of feeling on which he so prided himself, and which, when he spoke of his penury, prevented him from mentioning even once the sacrifices he had made for Tristana's family. That night, he felt an urge to settle accounts as regards gratitude, but the words died on his lips, and he merely thought to himself: *Don't forget that most of my fortune was eaten up by your parents. And can that not be weighed and measured too? Am I purely guilty? Do you not think that something should be placed on the other pan of the scales? Is this a fair way to weigh and to judge?*

"Fine," he said out loud, after a pause, during which he judged and assessed his captive's coldness, "you clearly do not want to tell me about your romance, but you're a fool, because you are telling me about it even without speaking, by the obvious repugnance you feel for me. Well, that's fine, my dear," he said, removing her from his lap and standing up. "Frankly, I'm not accustomed to arousing feelings of disgust in other people, nor with having to make so many requests in order to receive what is my due. I have more pride than that. What did you think? That I was going to get down on my knees and beg? Keep your youthful charms for one of the feeble young fellows you get nowadays, the sort one cannot call a man without belittling the word or raising the fellow up to ridiculous heights. Go to your room and think about what we have said. It might be that your romance will turn out to be a matter of complete indifference to me ... I could see it as an easy way for you to learn by experience the gulf that can exist between one man and another ... But it might well be, too, that it sticks in my gullet and that, without getting overly worked up about it, for the matter hardly merits it—why, it's like crushing ants—I may have to teach you the lesson myself."

So incensed was Tristana by this threat—which she must have found extraordinarily insolent—that she felt, rising up in her breast, the usual sense of loathing her tyrant aroused in her. And as always, when she experienced those tumultuous feelings, her cowardice instantly vanished and she felt strong enough to confront him, and attack him with a valiant riposte.

"You don't frighten me, you know. Kill me if you want."

And seeing her leave the room in that determined, arrogant fashion, Don Lope clutched his head and said to himself, "She clearly isn't afraid of me anymore. So my suspicions were right."

Meanwhile, Tristana ran to the kitchen in search of Saturna, and after much whispering and many tears, she issued her orders, which were more or less as follows: "Tomorrow, when you go to collect his letter, tell him not to bring the carriage and not to go out, but to wait for me in his studio, because I'll be there even if it kills me . . . Oh, and tell him to send his model away, if he has one tomorrow, and to receive no one else . . . he must be alone. If that man does kill me, then at least he'll have good reason to."

13

AND FROM that day on, they no longer went for walks.

They did, however, stroll about in the brief field of his studio, from the pole of the ideal to that of reality; they traveled the whole globe, from the human to the divine, never quite able to determine the dividing line between the two, because the human seemed to them the very stuff of heaven, and the divine, in their eyes, clothed itself in mortal flesh. When their joyful intoxication allowed Tristana to take in the world in which she spent those sweet hours, a new aspiration revealed itself to her spirit: art, which up until then had been merely a dream to her, but which now she could see and understand at first hand. Her imagination lit up and her eyes were enchanted by the human and inanimate forms that her lover translated from Nature and with which she filled his studio; and although she had seen paintings before, she had never observed how they were made from such close quarters. She would stick her finger into the fresh paint, thinking that she would thus gain a better appreciation of the secrets of the painted picture and catch it in the midst of its mysterious gestation. After watching Horacio work, she was even more captivated by that delicious art, which seemed so simply done, and she herself felt a desire to try her own skills. He placed a palette in her left hand, a brush in her right, and encouraged her to copy something. At first, alas, amid much laughter and frustration, she could only cover the canvas with shapeless blotches; on the second day, amazingly enough, she managed to mix a few colors and apply them to the right spot and even blend them together rather well. How funny! What if she turned out to be a painter too! She clearly had talent, for her hand became less clumsy by the hour, and if her hand couldn't help her, then her mind would march arrogantly ahead of her, knowing *how it was done*, even though she couldn't actually do it. Disheartened by the difficulties encountered, she would grow impatient, and Horacio would laugh, saying, "It's not a game, you know!"

She complained bitterly because she had never had at her side people who might have been able to recognize her aptitude and encourage her to apply it to the study of one art form or another.

"It seems to me now that if I had been taught drawing when I was a child, I would be able to paint now and live independently, earning my own living from my honest labors. But it never occurred to my poor mama to give me anything more than the kind of insubstantial education intended to help girls bring a good son-in-law home, namely, being able to play the piano a little, having a smattering of French, and a few other such accomplishments. If they had at least taught me a few languages, so that, when I was left alone and poor, I could have become a language teacher! And that wretched man has educated me for nothing but idleness and his own pleasure, Turkish-fashion. And I am utterly useless. As you see, I love painting; I feel a real vocation for it, a facility. Or am I being immodest? No, don't tell me. Praise me, encourage me. Well, if difficulties are to be overcome with willpower, patience, and application, then I will overcome them, and I will be a painter, and we will study together and my paintings—you'll be green with envy!—will make yours look puny. No, that's not true, you are the very king of painters! Don't get annoyed with me; you are, because I say so. I have an instinct for these things. I may not know how to make the paintings myself, but I have excellent judgment."

These painterly ambitions, these arrogant outbursts, delighted kindly Horacio, who, shortly after their first intimate encounters, began to notice that while his young lover was growing in his eyes, he was shrinking in hers. This surprised him and *almost* began to irritate him, because he had imagined that Tristana would be his subordinate as regards intelligence and willpower, the sort of wife who lives off the moral and intellectual sap of her husband and who sees and feels with his eyes and heart. It turned out, however, that the young woman had her own ideas, hurling herself into the empty spaces of thought and displaying the boldest of aspirations.

"Look, love of my life," she would say to him during the long rambling conversations that propelled them from the transports of love to life's most serious problems, "I love you with all my heart, and I know that I could never live without you. Every woman aspires to marry the man she loves, but not me. According to society's rules, I cannot marry. I couldn't marry anyone, not even you, not with my head held high, because, however kind and good you might be, I would always have the uncomfortable feeling that I had given you less than you deserve, and I would be afraid that, sooner or later, in a moment of bad temper or tiredness, you would say to me that you'd had to close your eyes in order to make me your wife. Is that pride or something else? I love you and will always love you, but I want to be free. That's why I need to find a way of making a living. Difficult, isn't it? Saturna pokes fun at me. According to her, there are only three careers open to women: marriage, the theater, and...well, frankly, I don't fancy any of them. So we'll have to find another. But I wonder: Is it madness to have a talent and cultivate it and live by it? Do I understand so little of the world that I'm thinking what's possible is, in fact, impossible? You tell me, because you know more than I do."

And after much beating about the bush, Horacio, deeply embarrassed, would find himself agreeing with Saturna.

"But you," he would add, "you are an exception, and the rule doesn't apply to you. You will find the formula, you will perhaps resolve the prickly problem of the free woman—"

"Free and honorable, of course, because I don't think I am dishonoring myself by loving you, whether we live together or not. But now you'll tell me that I've lost all sense of morality."

"No, not at all. I believe—"

"I'm a very bad woman, you know. Be honest, now, weren't you a little frightened by what I just said. I've dreamed of that honorable freedom for a long time now, and I have a much clearer sense of that free and honorable life since I've been in love with you and now that my intelligence has awoken and I'm constantly being surprised by the winds of knowledge that blow through my mind like a draft through a half-open door. I think about it all the time, and think about you, and I can't help cursing the people who never taught me an art or even a trade, because if they had set me to stitching shoes, by now I would be a skilled worker, possibly a mistress of my trade. But I'm still young, don't you think? Now you're laughing at me. That means that I'm young for love, but too old to learn a skill. Don't worry. I will become young again, I'll slough off the years, I'll return to childhood and make up for lost time by sheer hard work. A strong will can overcome anything, don't you think?"

Captivated by such determination, Horacio became more loving with each day that passed, his love reinforced by admiration. Her exuberant imagination awoke in him new mental energies; the sphere of his ideas grew larger, and so infectious was that powerful combination of strong feelings and deep thoughts that together they reached new heights, experienced a tempestuous intoxication of the senses, filled with daringly utopian moments, both social and erotic. They philosophized with a rare freedom even as they exchanged wild endearments and caresses, and overcome by tiredness, they would talk languidly until they ran out of breath. Their mouths fell silent, but their spirits continued to flutter about in space.

Meanwhile, nothing worthy of note was happening in Tristana's relations with her master, who had adopted an expectant, observational stance, and while being particularly attentive to her, he abstained from any displays of affection. He would see her come home late on certain nights and observe her closely; but he did not reprimand her, sensing that, at the slightest hint of conflict, his slave would reveal her intention to declare her emancipation. On some evenings, they would talk about various topics, but Don Lope, with cold tactical skill, would avoid any mention of the "romance"; and she revealed such spirit, and her mother-of-pearl Japanese face was so transformed by her dark eyes bright with intelligence, that Don Lope, restraining his desire to cover her in kisses, would be filled with melancholy and say to himself, "She's really blossoming. She must be in love."

Quite often, he would find her in the dining room at unusual hours, sitting beneath the circle of light from the hanging lamp, copying a figure from an engraving or one of the objects in the room.

"Very good," he said to her on the third or fourth occasion on which he found her thus engaged. "You're making progress, my dear, you really are. I can see the difference between now and the night before last."

And shutting himself up in his room with his melancholy, the poor, declining gallant would thump his fist on the table and exclaim, "Another fact. The man is a painter."

But he did not want to make any direct investigations, finding such activities offensive to his sense of decorum and inappropriate to his never profaned knightliness. One afternoon, however, while he was standing on the platform of the tram talking to one of the conductors, who was a friend of his, he asked, "Is there an artist's studio around here, Pepe?"

At precisely that moment, they were passing the cross street formed by some new buildings intended for the poor, among which was a fine, large building of bare brick, topped off by a kind of glass house, like the studio of a photographer or artist.

"Up there," said the conductor, "we have Señor Díaz, a portrait painter in oils."

"Ah, yes, I know him," said Don Lope. "The one who—"

"The one who comes and goes each morning and each evening. He doesn't sleep here. A handsome fellow!"

"Yes, he's dark, isn't he, and rather slight?"

"No, he's tall."

"Ah, yes, tall, but a bit round-shouldered."

"No, he cuts a very elegant figure."

"And he has long hair."

"No, he wears his hair short."

"He's obviously had it cut recently. He looks like one of those Italians who play the harp."

"Well, I don't know about him playing a harp, but he certainly works hard with his brushes. He asked a colleague of ours to act as a model for one of the apostles and he got him to the life."

"I thought he did landscapes."

"Oh, that too, and horses. He paints flowers that look as if they were real and ripe fruit and dead quail. Well, a little of everything really. And the pictures of naked women he has in his studio really make you sit up."

"Naked girls, you say?"

"Or half undressed, with a bit of cloth that both covers and uncovers. Go up and see for yourself, Don Lope. He's a good chap Don Horacio, and he'll give you a warm welcome."

"I've seen it all before, Pepe. Those painted ladies do nothing for me. I've always preferred the flesh-and-blood variety myself. Anyway, goodbye for now."

14

It should be said that Horacio, that highly spiritual artist, overwhelmed by his intoxicatingly amorous encounters with Tristana, found himself diverted from his noble profession. He painted little and almost always without a model: He began to feel the remorse of the worker, the sorrow provoked by unfinished pieces crying out to be given final shape; however, presented with a choice between art and love, he chose love, because it was a new experience for him and awoke in his soul the sweetest of emotions, a newly discovered world, lush, exuberant, and rich, a world that demanded to be taken possession of and required the geographer and conquistador to plant his foot firmly upon it. Art could wait; he would return to it when his mad desire had died down a little, as it would, and love would then take on a more peaceful character, more suited to quiet colonization than to furious conquest. Good Horacio genuinely believed that this was the love of his life, that no other woman would ever be able to please him now or replace the impassioned and witty Tristana in his heart; and he consoled himself with the thought that time would temper her fever-pitch thinking, because such an outflow of bold ideas was excessive in a wife or an eternal beloved. He hoped that constant affection and time would whittle away at his idol's powers of imagination and reasoning, making her more feminine, more domestic, more ordinary and useful.

This is what he thought, but did not say. One night when they were talking, looking out at the sunset and savoring the sweet melancholy of a misty evening, Horacio was startled to hear her express herself in the following terms.

"It's very odd what's happening to me: I learn difficult things very easily; I can pick up the ideas and rules of an art or even, if you press me, a science, but I can't grasp the practical details of life. Whenever I buy something, I get swindled; I don't know the value of things; I have no idea about housework or order, and if Saturna didn't do everything at home, the place would be a complete mess. It's true that everyone has a role in life, and I could play many roles, but I'm clearly not cut out for domesticity. I'm like those men who have no idea how much a bag of potatoes costs or a sack of coal. Saturna has told me a hundred times, but it goes in one ear and out the other. Perhaps I was born to be a fine lady. Regardless of whether I was or not, though, I have to apply myself and learn those things, without neglecting my studies, of course, and find out how to take care of chickens and darn clothes. I do a lot of work at home, but never on my own initiative. I'm Saturna's scullery maid, and I do sweep and clean and scrub, but pity the poor house if I were in charge of it! But I have to learn, don't I? Old Don Lope didn't even bother to teach me that. I've never been anything but an exotic Circassian slave bought for his amusement, and it was enough for him that I was pretty, clean, and willing."

The painter told her not to worry about acquiring such domestic wisdom, she would soon learn when she had to.

"You're a young woman," he added, "with enormous talent and aptitude. All you lack are those minor details, the extra knowledge that comes with independence and necessity."

"My fear," said Tristana, throwing her arms about his neck, "is that you will stop loving me when you find out that I don't even know what five pesetas can buy and will start to feel afraid that I might turn the house upside down. The fact is that if I ever manage to paint like you or discover another profession in which I can shine and work in good faith, how are we going to manage, my love? It's frightening."

She expressed her alarm so sweetly that Horacio could not help but laugh.

"Don't worry, my dear, we'll be all right. I'll wear the skirts. What else can we do?"

"No, no," said Tristana, charmingly wagging her finger. "If I find a way of earning my own living, then I will live alone. Long live independence . . . although I will, of course, still love you and always be yours. I know what I want. I have my own ideas on the matter. There's to be no matrimony, so there will be no arguments about who wears the skirts and who doesn't. I think you would love me less if you made me your slave, and I think I would love you less if I had you under my thumb. Freedom with honor, that's my motto or, if you like, my dogma. I know it's difficult, very difficult to achieve, because of what Saturna calls *socighty* . . . Oh, I don't know. But I'm going to throw myself into the experiment. And if I fail, I fail, but if I don't, my darling, if I get my own way, what will you say then? There I will be alone in my own little house, loving you intensely, of course, and working, working at my art in order to earn my daily bread; and there you will be in your little house, and sometimes we'll be together and sometimes apart for whole hours, because this being together all the time, day and night, is slightly—"

"You are funny and I love you so very much! But I refuse to spend some of the day apart from you. We will be two in one, Siamese twins, and if you want to wear the trousers, fine, do so; if you want to be one of those mannish women, carry on. But there is a slight problem. Shall I tell you what it is?"

"Yes, tell me."

"No, I don't want to. It's too soon."

"What do you mean 'too soon'? Tell me or I'll bite your ear off."

"Well, do you remember what we were talking about last night?"

"Yeth."

"You don't."

"Of course I do, silly. I have an amazing memory. You said that in order to complete your dream, you wanted—"

"Go on, say it."

"No, you say it."

"I wanted to have a child."

"Oh, no, no. I would love the child so much that I would die of grief if God took it away from me. Because they do all die," she said passionately. "Haven't you seen the constant procession of little white coffins? It makes me so sad. I really don't know why God allows them to come into the world only to take them away so soon. No, no. A child born is a child dead . . . and ours would die too. It's best not to have any. Say we won't."

"No, I won't say that. Now really, why would it die? Suppose it were to live . . . that's where the problems would start. If we have to live apart, each in our own house, me independent and you free and honorable, each in our own household, utterly honorable and entirely and utterly free, where would our little angel live?"

Tristana remained thoughtful, staring at the lines of the floorboards. She hadn't been expecting to be confronted with such an awkward problem and could find no immediate way of resolving it. Suddenly, a whole world of ideas crowded in on her and she burst out laughing, confident that the truth was hers, a truth which she expressed thus: "Why, with me, of course, where else? If the child is mine, who else would it live with?"

"But it would be mine too, it would belong to both of us."

"Yes, it would be yours, but . . . no, I don't want to say it. All right, it would be yours, but it would be more mine than yours. No one could doubt that it was mine, because Nature tore it from me. Your part in it would be undeniable, but it wouldn't count for as much, as far as the world was concerned, I mean. Oh, don't make me talk about such things or give these explanations!"

"No, on the contrary, it's best to have it out in the open. If we found ourselves in that situation, I would say: It's mine."

"And, still more loudly, I would say: It's mine, eternally mine."

"And mine too."

"All right, but—"

"There are no buts about it."

"No, you don't understand. It would be your child too, of course, but it would belong more to me."

"No, it would be equally yours and mine."

"Nonsense, man, it could never be equally yours and mine. You see, there might be cases when, and I'm speaking generally now—"

"No, let's stick to the particular."

"Well, then, speaking particularly, I say that the child is mine and I won't let it go, so there!"

"Well, we'll see—"

"No, we won't."

"But it's mine, mine."

"Yes, yours, but what I mean to say is that this business of it being 'yours' isn't so very clear, not generally speaking. And besides, Nature gives me more rights than she does you. And it will have the same name as me, with my surname and nothing more. So why all the fuss?"

"How can you say that, Tristana?" Horatio said with a hint of irritation.

"You're not angry, are you? It's your fault. Why be ... No, please, don't be annoyed with me. I unsay everything I said."

The small cloud passed and immediately everything was once again sunshine and light in the briefly obscured heaven of their happiness. Horacio, nevertheless, still felt slightly sad. Tristana tried to dissipate that fleeting fear and, speaking more sweetly and bewitchingly than ever, said, "Fancy quarreling over such a remote possibility, which might never happen! Forgive me. I can't help it. I come out with ideas as easily as my face might come out in spots. Is it my fault? When I least expect it, I think things one shouldn't think. But pay no attention. Next time, you must simply beat me with a stick. Think of my latest outburst as a kind of mental or nervous illness to be cured with frequent applications of the cane. How foolish we are, getting all hot and bothered about something that doesn't even exist, that as far as we know may never exist, when the present moment is so easy and so nice. Let's just enjoy it while we can!"

15

YES, THE present moment was, indeed, easy and nice, and Horacio was deliriously happy in it, as if he had been transported to a corner of the eternal glory. He was, however, a serious man, brought up in thoughtful solitude and in the habit of gauging everything as a way of foreseeing how things might turn out. He wasn't the kind of man so easily intoxicated by joy that he would fail to see its reverse side. His clear understanding allowed him to analyze himself keenly and to examine his immutable self regardless of what deliriums or storms assailed it. The first thing he encountered during that analysis was the irresistibly seductive effect that this young Japanese lady exercised over him, a phenomenon that was like a sweet illness of which he did not wish to be cured. He considered it impossible to live without her multiple attractions, her ineffable sweetness, without the one thousand fascinating forms in which the divinity had clothed herself when she took on human shape. He was charmed by her modesty when she was humble and by her pride when she grew angry. He was as enchanted by her wild enthusiasms as by her disappointments or sorrows. She was as delicious when cheerful as when she was annoyed. She possessed innumerable gifts and qualities, some serious, others frivolous and worldly; sometimes her intelligence judged everything with searing clarity, at other times with seductive absurdity. She could be sweet and sour, soft and cool as water, hot as fire, vague and murmurous as the air. She would invent amusing pranks, donning the clothes worn by his models and improvising monologues or whole plays in which she played two or even three characters; she would give witty discourses or mimic old

Don Lope; in short, she was the embodiment of such talent and such wit that Horacio, who was hopelessly in love, thought that his young friend was a compendium of all the gifts bestowed on mortal beings.

In the field, if one can call it that, of loving tenderness, Tristana was equally prodigious. She was able to find ever new ways of expressing her affection; she could be sweet without being sickly, guileless without being insipid, bold without a hint of corruption, and the first and most visible of her infinite graces was her utter sincerity. And seeing in her something that hinted at the precious virtue of constancy, Horacio believed that their mutual passion would last all their lives and possibly beyond, because, as a genuine believer, he did not think that his ideal would be plunged into the dark by death.

In the midst of all this eternal passion and growing ardor, art was the loser. In the morning, Horacio would amuse himself painting flowers or dead animals. His lunch would be brought up to him from the Café del Riojano, and he would devour it hungrily, arranging any leftovers on one of the tables in the studio. The latter was a delightfully untidy place, and the concierge, who tried to restore order each morning, only added to the confusion and disorder. There were piles of books on the wide divan and a blanket from Morella; on the floor lay boxes of paint, flowerpots, and dead partridges; on the bentwood chairs sat unfinished paintings, more books, and portfolios of prints; in the small adjoining room, which served as bathroom and storeroom, there were more small paintings, a water jug full of foliage cut from bushes, one of Tristana's dressing gowns hanging from a hook, and, scattered everywhere, beautiful costumes: a white woolen Moorish cloak, a Japanese robe, masks, gloves, and embroidered frock coats, wigs, harem slippers, and Roman peasant girls' aprons. The walls were adorned with chasubles and Greek masks made of cardboard, along with hundreds of portraits and photographs of horses, ships, dogs, and bulls.

After lunch, Díaz waited for half an hour and, when his beloved did not appear, he grew impatient and, to pass the time, sat down to read Leopardi. He knew Italian perfectly, for his mother had taught him, and although under his grandfather's long tyranny, he had forgotten a few turns of phrase, the roots of that knowledge lived on in him, and in Venice, Rome, and Naples, he had become so proficient that he could easily pass for an Italian anywhere, even in Italy itself. Dante was his one literary passion. He could recite, without forgetting a single line, whole cantos of the *Inferno* and *Purgatory*. Needless to say, almost without intending to, he gave his young friend lessons in *il bel parlare*. With her prodigious assimilatory powers, Tristana mastered the pronunciation in a matter of days and simply by reading occasionally as if for her own amusement and hearing him read too, within a fortnight she was reciting, with the admirable intonation of a consummate actress, the famous passages about Francesca, Ugolino, and others.

As I was saying, Horacio was whiling away the time reading that melancholic poet from Recanati and had paused to ponder the profound thought *E discoprendo, solo il nulla s'accresce,** when, hearing the light steps he was longing to hear, he immediately forgot all about Leopardi and cared little whether *il nulla* grew or shrank.

Thank heavens! Tristana entered with a childlike agility undiminished even by the weariness of climbing that interminable staircase, and she ran straight to him and embraced him as if she had not seen him for a year.

"My love, my sweet, my joy, my dauber, what a long time it seems since yesterday! I was longing to see you again. Have you been thinking about me? I bet you didn't dream about me as I did of you. I dreamed that . . . no, I won't tell you. I want to make you suffer."

"You're worse than a fever, you are! Give me those luscious lips of yours, if you don't, I'll strangle you!"

"Tyrant, pirate, gypsy!" she cried and fell, exhausted, onto the divan. You're not going to get around me with your *parlare onesto . . . Sella el labio . . . Denantes que del sol la crencha rubia . . .* Goodness me, what nonsense I talk! Pay no attention. I'm mad, and that's en-

---

*"Discovery reveals that only nothingness grows": from Leopardi's poem "Ad Angelo Mai."

tirely your fault. Oh, I have so many things to tell you, *carino*! Italian is so beautiful, so sweet, how pleasing to the soul it is to say *mio diletto*! I want you to teach me properly so that I can be a teacher too. But to business. Before we do anything else, answer me this: "*Shall we scarper?*"

It was clear from this mixture of street jargon and Italian words, along with other oddities of style that will emerge later on, that they shared a special lovers' vocabulary composed of all kinds of words culled from picaresque anecdotes or jokes, or from some very serious literary passage or famous line of poetry. It is precisely such accidental linguistic encounters that enrich the family dictionary of those who live in an absolute communion of ideas and feelings. The phrase "shall we scarper" came from a story Saturna had told her, and was a cheerful way of referring to their plans to run away together; and Tristana's habit of never addressing him by his name, but as Señó Juan—a coarse, ill-tempered gypsy—came from a funny tale Horacio had told her. Putting on the gruffest voice she could manage, Tristana would seize him by the ear and say, "So, Señó Juan, do you love me?"

He rarely called Tristana by her real name either. She was either Beatrice or Francesca,* or else la Paca de Rimini, or even Chispa or Señá Restituta. These nicknames, grotesque terms, or lyrical expressions, which lent savor to their passionate conversations, changed every few days, depending on the anecdotes they told each other.

"We can scarper whenever you wish, my dear Restituta," answered Horacio. "That is my one desire. A man can only take so much ecstatic love. Let us go: 'Why waste time? The dapple-gray mare which, as you say, graces the fields...'"†

---

*A reference to Francesca di Rimini in Dante's *Inferno*, who was damned for her illicit affair with the handsome brother of her deformed husband. The lovers create endless variations on their pet names for each other: Paca, Paquita, Panchita, Frasquita, Curra, Currita de Rimini—which recur throughout their letters and conversations.

†A line from a play by the Duque de Rivas, from the scene in which Don Álvaro is about to elope with Leonor, who hesitates because of her feelings for her father.

"Abroad, I will abroad!" she exclaimed, clapping her hands. "I want us both to be foreigners somewhere so that we can walk around, arm in arm, without anyone knowing who we are."

"Yes, my love. *What a joy it is to see you!*"

"Among the French," she sang, "and among the English . . . I don't think I can stand my own personal Tyrant of Syracuse for very much longer. Saturna calls him Don Lepe,* and so that's what I call him too. He's trying very hard to look pathetic. He barely speaks to me, which I don't mind at all. He's putting on an act, hoping that I'll feel sorry for him. He was very chatty last night, though, and regaled me with some of his 'adventures.' The rogue probably thinks he can impress me with such examples, but he's wrong. I can't stand the sight of him. Oh, there are days when I feel sorry for him, but on others, I loathe him, and last night I loathed him, because when he was telling me about his sordid escapades—they would make your hair stand on end—I sensed a depraved intention on his part to excite my imagination. He's a sly dog. I felt like telling him that the only 'adventure' I'm interested in is my own adventure with my beloved Señó Juan, whom I adore with all my 'irrational powers.'"

"You know, I would rather like to hear Don Lope recounting his amorous tales."

"They're pretty good. The one about the Marquesa del Cabañal is the funniest of all! She was led to Don Lepe by her own husband, who was more jealous than Othello himself. But I think I've told you that one before. Then there was the nun he kidnapped from the convent of San Pablo in Toledo. And that same year, he killed a man in a duel, a general who claimed his wife was the most virtuous woman in Spain; said wife promptly eloped with Don Lope to Barcelona, where he had seven affairs in a month, each one of them worthy of a novel. He must have something about him, and he doesn't lack for courage either."

"Don't get too excited about your Don Juan, Restituta."

Saber más que Lepe ("to know more than Lepe") is an idiom meaning "to be very shrewd."

"The only man I get excited about is my dauber here. I have such bad taste! Look at those eyes—so ugly, so dull! And that mouth? It makes one sick to look at it, and those clothes, so inelegant! I don't know how I can bear to look at you! No, it's too much. Get out of my sight this instant!"

"And what about you? With those huge tusks of yours and that beetroot of a nose and that barrel of a body! Your fingers are like pincers!"

"All the better to tear off your donkey pelt strip by strip. Why are you so ugly! *Gran Dio, morir si giovine.*"*

"Ah, my angel, lovelier than all the Holy Fathers and more bewitching by far than the Council of Trent and Don Alfonso the Wise ... Do you know what I have just thought? What if your Don Lepe were to come through that door right now?"

"Oh, you don't know Don Lepe. He would never come here, he wouldn't play the jealous husband for all the money in the world. Apart from having seduced a lot of more or less virtuous women, he is the very epitome of dignity."

"And what if I were to go to your house at night and he were to find me there?"

"Then, purely as a preventative measure, he might well slice you in two or turn your skull into a box in which to store the bullets from his revolver. He may be a gentleman to his fingertips, but if someone were to touch a raw nerve, he could react very violently. So it would be best not to go. I don't know how he found out about us, but he did. The rascal knows about everything, well, he's as wise as a wily old dog and has long experience as a master of naughtiness. Yesterday, he remarked very sarcastically: 'So we've found ourselves a little artist, have we?' I didn't answer. I pay no attention. One fine day, he'll arrive home and find that the bird has flown. *Ahi Pisa, vituperio de le genti!*† Where shall we go, my love? *A dó* will you take

---

*"Dear God! To die so young!": from Violetta's aria in act 3 of Verdi's *La Traviata*.
†"Ah, Pisa, shame of the people!": from Dante's *Inferno*, canto 33, line 79.

me? *La ci darem la mano...** I know I'm not making any sense. Ideas rush pell-mell into my head, arguing about who should go first, rather as if lots of people were trying to leave church at once and got stuck in the doorway and ... Oh, just love me, love me profusely, for everything else is mere noise. Sometimes I have sad ideas, for example, that I will end up very unhappy and see all my dreams of happiness go up in smoke. That's why I cling to the idea of gaining my independence and doing something with whatever talent I may have. If I really do have a gift, why shouldn't I put it to good use, just as other women exploit their beauty or their grace?"

"That is a most noble wish," said Horacio thoughtfully. "But don't be in such a hurry, don't cling too hard to that ambition, because it might prove impracticable. Give yourself unreservedly to me. Be my life's companion; help and sustain me with your love. Could there be a more beautiful trade or art? Making happy the man who will make you happy? What more could you want?"

"What more could I want?" she asked, staring down at the floor. *"Diverse lingue, orribile favelle...parole di dolore, accenti d'ira...†* Not that I'm comparing, of course ... Señó Juan, do you really love me? You asked me: 'What more?' Well, nothing more. I will accept that there is nothing more. I warn you, though, that I'm an absolute disaster as a housewife. I get everything wrong and I'll cause you all kinds of upsets. And I'm an equally perfect treasure, too, when it comes to shopping and other such women's business. I need only tell you that I don't know the names of the streets and can't go out alone without getting lost! The other day, I couldn't even manage to get from Puerta del Sol to Calle de Peligros, found myself heading off in completely the wrong direction and ended up in Plaza de la Cebada. I have no sense of direction at all. That same day, I bought some hairpins at the market, gave the stallholder five pesetas, and forgot to

---

* "There we give each other our hands": from the aria in act 1 of Mozart's *Don Giovanni.*

†"Tongues confused, a language strained in anguish, with cadences of anger, shrill outcries": from Dante's *Inferno,* canto 3, lines 25–26, describing the entrance to hell.

take the change. By the time I realized my mistake, I was already on the tram . . . I even caught the wrong tram and got one going to El Barrio. From all these things and something else that I observe in myself, I deduce . . . But tell me what you're thinking about? Will you really never love anyone more than you love your Paquita de Rimini? I'll say it again . . . No, I won't."

"Finish your sentence," he said, feeling rather uncomfortable. "I must cure you of that annoying habit of never finishing a thought."

"Beat me, beat me, then . . . break a rib or two. You have such a temper! 'Nor golden ceiling made by the wise Moor and supported on pillars of jasper . . .' No, that doesn't make sense either."

"Well, what does, then?"

"All right, *Inés, I'll explain how it is* . . . Listen," she said, holding him tightly in her arms. "Having studied myself in depth, because I do study myself, you know, I have come to the conclusion that I am only good at the big things and decidedly bad at the small things."

Horacio's response was lost in the ensuing wave of tender caresses that filled the quiet solitude of the studio with murmurings.

16

As a moral and physical counterweight to those exalted afternoons and evenings, Horacio, when he returned home at night, would collapse upon the dark breast of a melancholy that was either utterly devoid of ideas or filled only with the very vaguest of thoughts, with an indefinable languor and anxiety. What was wrong? It wasn't easy for him to find an answer. Ever since the days of his slow martyrdom at the hands of his grandfather, he had periodically suffered acute attacks of spleen, which resurfaced during any abnormal episode in his life. Not that he grew weary of Tristana during those secluded hours or was left with a bitter aftertaste from all the sweetnesses of the day, no, the image of her pursued him; the fresh memory of her many attractions set him trembling, and far from seeking an end to such ardent emotions, he longed to repeat them, fearing that they might one day desert him. Although he considered his fate to be inseparable from the fate of that remarkable woman, a dumb terror stirred in the depths of his soul, and however hard he tried, forcing his imagination to its very limits, he simply could not imagine spending the future at Tristana's side. His idol's grand aspirations amazed him, but when he tried to follow her along the paths that she revealed to him with such graceful tenacity, her bewitching figure disappeared into some nebulous nothingness.

Doña Trinidad (the aunt with whom Horacio lived) was, at first, unperturbed by her nephew's melancholy, until she noticed in him a worrying indifference and indolence. He fell into a kind of waking torpor, and it was impossible to get a word out of him. He would sit motionless in his armchair in the dining room, paying not the slightest heed to the chatter of the few guests who brightened Doña Trini's sad evenings. She was a very sweet lady, and although not yet old, she was in perennially poor health and weighed down by the many sorrows that had burdened her life, for she found no peace until she was left with no father and no husband. She blessed her solitude and felt she owed a large debt of gratitude to death.

Her troubled existence had left her with a nervous debility, a slackening of the muscles around the eyelids. She could only half open her eyes and on certain days or in certain weathers, she could do so only with some difficulty, and when the condition was at its worst, she sometimes had to lift her own eyelids with her fingers in order to see a person clearly. She also suffered from a very weak chest, and as soon as winter set in, she would be in a terrible state, coughing and wheezing, her feet and hands icy, her one thought being how best to defend both herself and the house against the cold. She adored her nephew and would not for the world have been parted from him. One night, after supper and before her guests had arrived, Doña Trini sat down, all hunched, opposite the armchair in which Horacio was sitting, smoking, and said, "If it wasn't for you, I wouldn't be able to withstand this wretched winter cold. It will be the death of me one day. Now if I were to go to your house in Villajoyosa, I would revive at once, but how could I leave you here all alone? Impossible, quite impossible!"

Her nephew replied that she could easily go and leave him there, for no one would eat him.

"Who knows, perhaps they would! You're not well yourself. No, I won't go, I won't be parted from you for anything in the world."

From that night on there began a stubborn struggle between the aunt's desire to travel and her nephew's sedentary passivity. Doña Trini longed to leave Madrid; he wanted her to leave as well, because the Madrid climate was rapidly undermining her health. He would have liked to accompany her, but how, dear God, when he could see no human way of loosening, let alone breaking the amorous chain keeping him there?

"I'll take you there," he told his aunt, hoping to negotiate, "then come straight back."

"No, that won't do."

"I'll come and fetch you in early spring."

"No, that won't do either."

Doña Trini's stubbornness had its roots in more than just her horror of winter, which was advancing that year with sword in hand, for while she knew nothing specific about Horacio's love life, she suspected that something abnormal and dangerous was going on, and her instincts told her this would be a good moment to take him away from Madrid. That night her eyelids were worse than usual, her vision diminished by about two-thirds, but raising her head so that she could look at him properly, she said, "It seems to me that you would paint just as well in Villajoyosa as you do here, if not better. You can find Nature and the natural world everywhere. More important, down there you would be able to slough off all your current problems and anxieties. I'm telling you this as someone who truly cares for you and knows what this treacherous world is like. There is nothing worse than becoming unhealthily attached to someone. Cut the tie now. Distance is the best remedy."

Having said that, Doña Trini allowed her eyelids to droop again, like an embrasure closing once the shot has been fired. Horacio said nothing, but his aunt's words stayed in his mind like seeds preparing to germinate. The kindly widow repeated her wise exhortations the following night and, two days later, the painter no longer found the idea of leaving so very foolish, nor did he now perceive a separation from his beloved as being as grave an occurrence as the planet breaking into a thousand pieces. He suddenly felt a kind of itch deep down inside him, a demand to rest. His whole existence was crying out for a truce, one of those parentheses which, in love and war, are deemed essential if lovers and combatants are to continue living and fighting.

The first time he told Tristana about Doña Trini's wishes, Tristana screamed blue murder. He, too, grew angry, and they both protested at the very idea of that importunate journey...better to die than give in to tyrants. But the next day, when they spoke of it again, Tristana seemed quite resigned. She felt sorry for the poor widow. It was only natural that she would prefer not to travel alone! Horacio agreed that Doña Trini would not withstand the rigors of the Madrid winter or accept being separated from her nephew. Tristana appeared more compassionate and, who knows, perhaps her body and soul were also crying out for a truce, a parenthesis, an interruption. Their mutual desire did not wane in the least, but a separation no longer frightened them; on the contrary, knowing that it would only be for a short time, they were keen to experience the as yet unknown charm of being apart, the taste of absence, with all its disquiets, the waiting for and receiving of letters, the reciprocal longing to see each other again, the counting off of the days until they could be together again.

In short, Horacio took to his heels. They bade each other a tender farewell: they had mistakenly believed that they had sufficient serenity of mind to withstand it, but, in the end, they felt like two condemned men before the scaffold. Once he was on his way, however, Horacio, to be honest, did not feel overly sad; he breathed more easily, like a laborer on a Saturday evening, after a week of working his fingers to the bone; he savored the moral repose, the somewhat dull pleasure of feeling no strong emotions. The first day in Villajoyosa, nothing of note happened. He felt perfectly satisfied and comfortable in his exile. On the second day, however, the tranquil sea of his mind began to stir and grow choppy, and the mounting waves grew rougher. After four days, he felt horribly lonely, sad, and deprived. Everything bored him: the house, Doña Trini, their relatives. He sought solace in art, but art brought him only dejection and rage. The beautiful countryside, the blue sea, the picturesque rocks, the wild pine woods made him scowl. Her first letter consoled him in his solitude; it was filled with the sweet pain of absence and that old cliché *nessun maggior dolore**... as well as the vocabulary they had forged together in their long, loving conversations. They

---

*"There is no greater pain [than to remember a happy time when one is in misery]": from Dante's *Inferno*, canto 5, line 121.

had agreed initially that they would write two brief letters a week, but this turned into *a daily letter every day* as Tristana put it. If his letters burned, hers positively scalded. An example:

"Yesterday was the cruelest of days and last night the foulest of nights, worthy of all the dogs in Satan's pack of hounds. Why did you leave? I feel calmer today though; I went to hear mass and prayed a lot. I realized that I mustn't complain, that I must restrain my egotism. God has given me so many good things and I mustn't be so demanding. You should tell me off and beat me and even love me a little less (no, please don't do that!), when I get so upset over such a brief and necessary absence. You tell me to calm down, and I am much calmer. *Tu duca, tu maestro, tu signore.** I know that my Señó Juan will come back soon, that he will always love me, and his Paquita de Rimini waits confidently, resigned to her *solichewed . . .*"

From him to her:

"What a day I've had! I tried to paint a donkey and what I produced was something resembling a wineskin with ears. I'm at my wit's end: I can't see color or line, all I can see is my Restituta, who lights up my eyes with her love for me. The image of my savage *monster* pursues me day and night, wilier than the Holy Spirit and more efficacious than all the salt in the *pharmasea*." [Editor's note: *Pharmasea* means *sea*, after an Andalusian story about a ship's doctor who treated everything with salt water.]

"My aunt is not well. I can't leave her. If I committed such a barbaric act, you yourself would never forgive me. My boredom is one terrible torment that our friend Alighieri neglected to write about . . .

"I've just reread your letter from Thursday, the one about paper birds, the one about ecstasies . . . *inteligenti pauca*—a word to the wise . . . When God launched you into the world, he clutched his august head, overwhelmed by regret and sorrow at having spent on you all the wit he had saved up to make a hundred generations. Please

---

*"You are my leader, my master, my teacher": from Dante's *Inferno*, canto 2, line 140.

don't tell me that you are worthless, that you are a zero. *I'm* the zero. I say unto you, even if it makes you blush as furiously as an aurora borealis, I say unto you, O my Restituta, that compared with you, all the good things in the world are not worth one *céntimo*; and all the glories of humanity dreamed up by ambition and pursued by fortune, are *an old shoe* compared with the glory of being your lord and master...I wouldn't change places with anyone...No, I take that back. I would like to be Bismarck so that I could create an empire and make you its empress. My love, I will be your humble vassal: Stamp on me, spit on me and order me to be whipped."

From her to him:

"Don't even joke about my Señó Juan ever ceasing to love me. You obviously don't know your Panchita de Rimini, who is not afraid of death and feels brave enough to *suicide herself* as elegantly as you like. I would kill myself as easily as someone drinking a glass of water. How delightful, how stimulating to one's curiosity! To find out at last what lies beyond and to see the face of the *pusultra*! To be cured once and for all of that annoying little question *to be or not to be*, as Shikespeer put it! So no more telling me that you love me a little less, because...if you could see Don Lepe's fine collection of revolvers...And I can use them too, you know, and if I get cross, bang, I'll be sleeping out the siesta with the Holy Spirit..."

And the wheels on the mail carriage of the train that carried this cargo of sentimentalism back and forth did not catch fire nor did the engine travel any faster, like a steed driven onwards by red-hot spurs! All that ardor lay hidden on the paper on which it was written.

17

TRISTANA'S moods were so changeable and so vehement that she passed easily from unfettered, epileptic joy to dark despair. Here is an example:

"*Caro bene, mio diletto*, is it true that you love and esteem me so very much? I can hardly believe it's true. Tell me, do you really exist or are you nothing but an empty phantasm, the child of my fevered imagination, of the dreams of beauty and greatness that trouble my mind? Please be so kind as to send me a supplementary letter just to reassure me or a telegram saying: *I exist. Signed, Señó Juan.* I'm so happy that sometimes I feel as if I were suspended in midair, as if my feet didn't touch the ground, as if I could smell eternity and breathe the breeze that blows somewhere up there beyond the sun. I can't sleep, but then what need of sleep have I? I want to spend the whole night thinking about how much I love you and counting the minutes until I see your precious face again. Are the Just who sit in ecstasy at the right hand of the Holy Trinity as happy as me? No, they're not, they can't be . . . There's only one thing that stands in the way of me and absolute happiness, one tiny, bothersome fear, like the speck of dust that gets in your eye and makes you suffer so horribly. And that is the suspicion that you do not yet love me enough, that you have not yet reached the outer limit of loving—but why speak of limits, when there are none—the threshold of the final heaven, because I never tire of asking for more, always more, I want only infinite things, you see, it's either the infinite or nothing. How many hugs do you think I will give you when you come home? Start counting. As many as the seconds it would take an ant to walk around the globe. No, more, far more. As many seconds as it would take an ant to split the globe in two with its little feet, trudging round and round on the same line. I leave it up to you to make the calculations, my little fool."

And another day:

"I don't know what's wrong with me, I'm beside myself with anxiety and fear. Since yesterday I have done nothing but imagine misfortunes and disasters: that you die, for example, and Don Lope comes to tell me the news with a joyful smile on his face, or that I die and they put me in that horrible coffin and throw earth on top of me. No, no, I don't want to die, I really don't. I don't want to know about the beyond, it doesn't interest me. I hope they resuscitate me and restore my dear little life to me. I hate the thought of my own skeleton. I hope they give me back my nice, young flesh along with all the kisses you've planted on it. I don't want to be nothing but cold bones and, later, dust. No, that's just a trick. I don't like the idea of my spirit going from star to star asking for hospitality or having a bald, irascible Saint Peter slam the door in my face. Because even if I were certain of being allowed into Paradise, I still don't want to hear about death. I want my life and the earth on which I've known both pain and pleasure, and where my naughty Señó Juan lives. I don't want wings, large or small, nor to live among a lot of boring, harp-plucking angels. You can keep the harps and accordions and the celestial lights. Give me life, health, and love and everything I desire.

"I find the problem of my life more overwhelming the more I think about it. I want to be somebody in the world, to cultivate an art, to live by my own means. I'm so easily discouraged. Am I really attempting the impossible? I want to have a profession, and yet I'm useless, I know nothing about anything. It's just awful.

"My ambition is to not have to depend on anyone, not even on the man I adore. I don't want to be his mistress—so undignified—or a woman maintained by a few men purely for their amusement, like a hunting dog; nor do I want the man of my dreams to become a husband. I see no happiness in marriage. To put it in my own words, I want to be married to myself and to be my own head of the household. I wouldn't know how to love out of obligation; I can only promise constancy and endless loyalty in a state of total freedom. I feel like protesting against men, who have appropriated the whole world for themselves and left us women only the narrowest of paths to take, the ones that were too narrow for them to walk along...

"I'm being boring, aren't I? Pay no attention. What ravings! I have no idea what I'm thinking or writing; my head is a hotbed of nonsense. Poor me! Pity me, make fun of me... Tell them to put me in a straitjacket and lock me in a cage. I can't give you any jokes today, I'm simply not in the mood. All I can do is cry, and this piece of paper carries with it a *pharmasea* of tears. Why was I born, tell me that. Why didn't I just stay out there, in the lap of Lady Nothingness, so beautiful, so tranquil, so sleepy, so...? I don't know how to end."

While these stormy winds were traveling the long distance between the Mediterranean town of Villajoyosa and Madrid, a crisis was brewing inside Horacio, the work of the inexorable law of adaptation, which first had to find the right conditions in which to operate. He loved the mildness of the climate, and the charms of the countryside finally opened up a path, if one can put it like that, through the fog shrouding his soul. Art conspired with Nature to win him over and having, one day, after many fruitless attempts, managed to paint a superb seascape, he remained forever bound to the blue sea, the luminous beaches, and the smiling face of the earth. The landscapes near and far, the town's picturesque amphitheater, the almond trees, the many faces of farmworkers and sailors all filled him with an intense desire to transpose it onto canvas; he began to work feverishly, and time, which had seemed so long-drawn-out and tedious, now became brief and fleeting, so much so that, after a month of living in Villajoyosa, the mornings ate up the afternoons and the afternoons the evenings and the evenings devoured the nights, and the artist sometimes forgot to eat.

He also began to feel the instinctive bond of the homeowner, the same nameless attraction that keeps the plant rooted in the soil and the spirit anchored in small domestic trifles. He owned the beautiful house in which he was living with Doña Trini, but it took him a whole month to begin to appreciate its comforts and its delightful situation. The vegetable garden, populated with ancient fruit trees, some very rare and all beautifully preserved, was also his, as were the strawberry patch, the asparagus bed, and the lush vegetable plots; his was the swift, abundant stream that flowed through the garden and surrounding fields. Not far from the house, he could also view with proprietorial eyes a stand of elegant palm trees of biblical beauty and an austere olive grove, full of gnarled, warty specimens like those in the garden of Gethsemane. When he wasn't painting, he went for long walks in the company of the simple village folk, and his eyes never wearied of contemplating the vast expanse of blue sky, the ever-admirable *pharmasea*, which changed its color from moment to moment, like a vast sentient being, infinitely impressionable. The lateen sails, sometimes white, sometimes burnished gold, added piquant touches to the majesty of that grandiose element, which, on some afternoons, looked milky and drowsy, on others choppy and transparent, revealing along its quiet shores crystalline, emerald-green shoals.

Needless to say, everything that Horacio saw was immediately communicated to Tristana.

From him to her:

"Ah, my love, you have no idea how beautiful it is here! But how could you when, until only recently, I myself was blind to such beauty and poetry? I so admire and love this corner of the planet, thinking that one day we will love and admire it together. But what am I saying? You *are* here, because I carry you within me, and I am sure that your eyes see what my eyes see! Ah, Restitutilla, how you would love my house, *our* house, if you were to see it! It's not enough that you are here in spirit. In spirit! Pure rhetoric, my love, that fills the lips but leaves the heart empty. Come and you will see for yourself. Resolve once and for all to leave that absurd old man and let us be married before this incomparable altar or before whatever other altar the world assigns to us, and which we will accept in order to keep the world happy... Do you know, I have told my illustrious aunt about us. I could keep the secret no longer. To my amazement, my dear, she didn't turn a hair. But even if she had, what difference would that make? I told her that I am devoted to you, that I cannot live without you, and she burst out laughing. How could she treat something so serious as a joke? But better that than grimaces. Tell me that you're pleased with my news and that when you read these words, it will make you want to come racing down here. Tell me that you have packed your trunks and are on your way. I don't know what my aunt would think of such an *impetulous* decision. Let her think what she likes. Tell me that you would enjoy this deliciously obscure life; that you would love this rustic peace; that here you would be healed of all the mad effervescences that trouble your mind; and that you long to be a happy, sturdy peasant—a wealthy bourgeois lady in the midst of all this simplicity and abundance—with, as your little husband, the maddest of artists, the most spiritual inhabitant of this land of light, fecundity, and poetry.

"Nota bene: I have a dovecote that tells the time, with thirty or more pairs of doves. I get up at dawn, and my first duty is to open their door. Out come my beloved friends, and to greet the new day, they fly about a little, tracing graceful spirals in the air; then they come and eat from my hand or strut around me, speaking to me in cooings, a language I regret to say I cannot translate for you. You would have to hear it and understand it for yourself."

18

From Tristana to Horacio:

"How very enthusiastic and silly my Señó Juan has grown! And how the glories of your new home have effaced all memory of the desert in which I live! You have even forgotten our vocabulary, and I am no longer Frasquita de Rimini. Well, well. I would like to be enthused by your *rusticicity* (you know how I like to invent words) *which makes one forget the gold and the scepter.* I do as you tell me, and I obey... insofar as I can. *It must be a beautiful country...* Imagine me as a peasant, keeping chickens, getting fatter by the day, more animal than human, and with a ring called *husband* through my nose! I will be a delight to the eyes and you an equally charming sight, with your early tomatoes and your late oranges, setting forth to gather prawns, and painting donkeys in baggy breeches or people in harness... no, the other way around. I can hear your doves from here and I understand their cooings. Ask them why I am so troubled by this mad ambition; why I want the impossible and always will, until the impossible itself stands in front of me and says: 'Can't you see me, you fool?' Ask them why I dream of being transported to another world, in which I will be free and honorable, loving you more than my own dear eyes... Enough, enough, *per pietà.* I'm drunk today. I have drunk down all your letters from the previous days and find them horribly full of cheap alcohol. You hoaxer!

"Fresh news! Don Lope, the great Don Lope, *before whom the Earth falls silent and prostrates itself,* is poorly. His rheumatism has taken it upon itself to avenge the innumerable husbands he cuckolded, as well as the honest virgins and vulnerable wives whom he sacrificed on the unspeakable altar of his lust. What a sad figure he cuts now! And yet I still feel sorry for this poor fallen Don Juan, because with the exception of his utterly shameless behavior toward women, he is kind and gentlemanly. Now that he walks with a limp and is no good for anything, he has suddenly resolved to understand me, to show some respect for my eagerness to learn a profession. Poor Don Lepe! Before, he used to make fun of me, now he applauds me and tears out the few hairs he has left on his head, furious that he did not understand earlier how reasonable my desires were.

"So, at considerable personal sacrifice, he has found me an English tutor, a woman, although you might well mistake her for one of the masculine gender or perhaps for neither one nor the other; she's a tall, bony, awkward woman, with a hideously ruddy face and a hat that looks like a birdcage. Her name is Doña Malvina and she previously worked in the evangelical chapel as a Protestant preacher, until they cut off her wages and she was obliged to give English lessons instead ... But wait until I tell you the really important news: My teacher says that I have an extraordinary gift for languages and is amazed that she only has to teach me something once for me to know it. She assures me that in six months I will know as much English as Chaskaperas or Lord Mascaole himself. And as well as teaching me English, she is refreshing my French, and then we will sink our teeth into German. *Give me a kiss*, you poltroon. I just don't know how you can be so *innorant* that you can't understand English.

"English is a very lovely language, almost as lovely as you, for you are like a fresh new rose in May ... if roses in May were as black as my shoes. Anyway, I am in a fever of activity. I study all the hours of the day and devour everything that I'm taught. Forgive my immodesty, but I can't help myself: I'm a prodigy. I'm amazed that I seem to know things as soon as they're shown to me. And by the way, Señó Juan, you of the orange trees and the baggy breeches, *Did you buy a steel nib pen from your neighbor's gardener's son?* Of course not, what you bought was *an ivory candlestick belonging to the mother-in-law of the* ... Sultan of Morocco.

"I nibble your ear. My regards to the doves. *To be or not to be...*
All the world's a stage."

From Señó Juan to Señá Restituta:

"Dearest lovekins, you little monkey, don't be such an intellectual. You frighten me. For my part, I would say that in my *rusticicity*
(new word duly accepted), I almost feel like forgetting the little I
know. Long live Nature! Down with Science! I would like to share
your hatred of the obscure life, *ma non posso*. My orange trees are
laden with blossoms—infuriating, isn't it?—and golden fruit. It does
one's heart good to see them. I have some chickens who, each time
they lay an egg, ask the heavens, cackling as they do so, why you
don't come and eat them. Their eggs are large enough to contain a
small elephant. The doves say they want nothing to do with the English, not even with those who hope to emulate the great *Shasspirr*.
Otherwise, they understand and practice honorable freedom and
free honor. I forgot to mention that I have three nanny goats with
udders the size of the drum they use to draw the lottery tickets from.
There is absolutely no comparison between their milk and the milk
they sell in the dairy next to your house, that *virginal, lacteal effusion*
we used to find so disgusting. The goats await you, my twopenny-
halfpenny Englishwoman, to offer you their *tumescent breasts*. Tell
me something...have you eaten any *turrón* this Christmas? I have
enough almonds and hazelnuts here to give you and all your tribe
indigestion. Come and I will show you how to make *turrón* from Ji-
jona and from Alicante and the really delicious sort they make with
egg yolk, although it could never be as sweet as your gypsy heart. Do
you like roast kid? I say this because if you were to eat it here, you
would be licking your fingers; no, I would lick those *fingles* for you,
for they are as precious as Saint John's pointing *forefingle*. You see, I
do remember the vocabulary. The *pharmasea* is rather rough today,
because the west wind is tickling it and making it nervous...

"As long as you don't get angry and call me prosaic, I must tell you
that I now eat enough for seven men. I adore roast garlic soup, salt

cod, and rice *in all its many guises*, turkey and red mullet with pine nuts. I drink gallons of that delicious water from Engedi or, rather, Aspe, and I am growing fat and even handsome, so that you will fall in love with me when you see me and delight in my charms or my *appas*, as we and the French say. What *appas* I have! And what about you? Please do not wither away with all that studying. I fear that Señá Malvina will infect you with her ugliness and her mannishness. Don't become too philosophical, don't climb up to the stars, because I'm much too fat now to climb up after you and pick you as I would pick a lemon from one of my trees. Don't you envy my way of life? What are you waiting for? If we don't do it now, when will we, *per Baco*? Please come. I'm preparing your room, which will be *manifissent*, a worthy setting for such a jewel. Say yes, is it such a labor (like that of the mountain that gave birth to a mouse) to say the word? Only say it and I will run and fetch you. *Oh donna di virtú!* Even if you become more of a know-it-all than Minerva herself and speak to me in Greek to make your meaning clearer; even if you know by heart the Pseudo-Isidorian Decretals and the logarithm tables, I will still adore you with all the force of my supine ignorance."

From Señorita Reluz:

"Such sorrow, such anxiety, such fear! I think only of dreadful things. I'm grateful to this foul cold I'm suffering from, because at least it gives me an excuse to be constantly dabbing at my eyes. Weeping consoles me. If you were to ask me why I'm crying, I wouldn't know how to answer. Ah, yes, I would. I'm weeping because I can't see you, because I don't know when I will see you again. Your absence is killing me. I'm jealous of that blue sea, the boats, the oranges, the doves, and fearful that all those lovely things will be what Galleot was for Lancelot and Guinevere. In a place full of so many good things, surely there must be pretty girls as well. Because for all my *knowitallness* (another of my invented words), I would kill myself if you were to leave me. You would be solely responsible for that tragedy...

"I have just received your letter. How it consoles me! In fact, it made me laugh out loud. I have recovered from my fit of spleen; I'm not crying anymore; I'm happy, so happy that I don't *knoo* how to express it. But don't try to impress me with your lemon trees and your *undulous stream*. As a free and honorable woman, I accept you as you are, a common rustic and a keeper of chickens. You are as you are, and I as I *are*. This idea that two people who love each other must become the same and think the same is quite simply inconceivable to me. Living one for the other! Two in one! What nonsense our egotism invents! Why this fusion of personalities? Let each be as God made him or her because, being different, they will love each other more. Leave me untethered, don't tie me up, don't erase my... shall I say it? Such big words stick in my throat, but, no, I'll say it anyway: my *idiosingrassee*.

"By the way, my teacher says that soon I will know more than she does. Pronunciation is my one stumbling block, but don't worry, I'll overcome it. This little tongue of mine will do whatever I tell it to. Bring on the clouds of incense! Such modesty! Anyway, I would have you know that I have mastered Grammar, I have devoured the Dictionary, my memory is as prodigious as my understanding (those are not my words, but Señá Malvina's). She's not one for jokes and believes that, with me, it's best to start at the end. And so, just like that, we have *plonged* into *Don Guillermo*, that immense poet, *the finest creator since God* according to Seneca... no, I mean Alexandre Dumas. Doña Malvina has her Shakespeare glossary by heart and knows the texts of all his plays like the back of her hand. She let me choose, and I chose *Macbeth*, because I've always found Lady Macbeth such a sympathetic character. She's my friend... Anyway, we immediately got to grips with that tragedy. The witches have *telled* me that I will be queen... and I believe them. Anyway, we're translating it as we go along. Oh, my love, that exclamation from Señá Macbeth, when she cries out to the heavens with all her heart *unsex me here*, it makes me tremble and awakens all kind of terrible emotions in the depths of my being! Since you are not a member of the *enlightened classes*, you will not understand what that means, and I will not explain because it would be like casting pearls... No, you are my heaven, my hell, my *magnettick* pole, and my compass needle is always pointing straight at you, your own dear servant, your... Lady Restitute."

Thursday, 14th

"Oh, I forgot to mention. The great Don Lope, *terror of families*, is all sweetness and light at the moment. He's still a martyr to his rheumatism, but has nothing but nice things to say to me. He's taken to calling me his daughter now, to relish the joy (or so he says) of calling himself my papa and to imagine that he really is. *E se non piangi, de che pianger suoli?** He regrets not having understood me better, not having cultivated my intelligence. He curses his negligence... But there's still time, we can still regain lost ground. I will have a profession that will allow me to be free and honorable; he will, if necessary, sell the shirt off his back. He has begun by bringing me a cartload of books, but since he has never had any in his house, they come from the library of his friend the Marquis de Cícero. Needless to say, I fell on them like a ravening wolf, first this one, then that, and I am positively stuffed with knowledge. Goodness, how much I *knoo*! In the space of eight days, I have swallowed more pages than you could buy lentils for five thousand pesetas. If you could see my little brain from inside, you would be frightened. Ideas are positively fighting for space in there. I have far too many of them and I don't know *wheech* ones to keep. I will as easily bite into a volume of History as into a treatise on Philosophy. I bet you don't know what Señor Leibniz's monads are. And no, I did not say *no-mads*. And if I come across a book on Medicine, I don't rear back from that either. No, I wade straight in. I want to know more and more and more. By the way... No, I won't tell you now. Another day. It's very late: I've stayed awake so as to write to you; *the pale torch of*

---

* "If you weep not now, when will you ever weep?": from Dante's *Inferno*, canto 33, line 42.

the moon is burning out, my love. I can hear the cock crowing, the *harbinger* of the new day, and already the sweet juice of henbane is flowing through my veins ... Go on, my rustic love, admit that the bit about henbane made you laugh. Anyway, I'm exhausted and am going to my *almo lecho*, my sacred couch, yes sir, and there'll be no turning back: *almo, almo*."

19

FROM HER to him:

"Dearest fool, why is it that the more I know—and I know a lot—the more I idolize you? Now that I'm rather ill and sad, I think about you even more. Now don't be so inquisitive, you want to know everything. It's nothing really, but it bothers me. Let's not talk about it. There's such a racket inside my head that I'm no longer sure if it really is my head or an insane asylum where they've locked up all the crickets who have lost their little cricket minds. I'm just utterly bewildered all the time, always thinking and thinking a thousand things, or rather millions of things, beautiful and ugly, large and small! Strangest of all is that your face has been quite erased from my memory: I cannot see your lovely face clearly; it's as if it were swathed in a mist that prevents me from making out your features or understanding your expression or your look. It's infuriating! Sometimes it seems to me that the mist clears... then I open the eyes of my imagination very wide and tell myself 'Now, now I'll see him,' but instead, I see even less, you grow still darker, you vanish completely, and farewell, my Señó Juan. You're becoming pure spirit, an intangible being, an... oh, I don't know how to describe it. When I consider what poor things words are, I feel like inventing lots more, so that I can say everything. Are you really you?

"I think everything you say about how dim-witted you've become is pure nonsense, designed to mislead me. No, my dear, you are a magnificent artist and carry the divine light in your brain; you will give Fame plenty to do and will amaze the world with your marvelous genius. I want people to say that, compared with you, Velázquez and Raphael were mere housepainters. They will, I promise. You're having me on, pretending to be a rustic, a seller of eggs, and an orange grower, when, in fact, you're silently working away and preparing a big surprise for me. They're not bad those eggs you're hatching! You're doing preparatory studies for the major painting that was your hope and mine, *The Embarkation of the Expelled Moriscos*, for which you have already done a few sketches. Please, do it, work on that. It's such a profoundly touching human drama! Hesitate no longer. Give up your hens and all other such foolish vulgarities. Art, glory, Señó Juanico! Art is the only rival I feel jealous of. Climb onto the horns of the moon: you can do it. If others are as capable as you are of watering the vegetables, why not apply yourself to something that only you can do? To each his own. And your business is divine art, in which you are not far off being a master. I have spoken."

Monday

"Shall I tell you? No, I won't. You'll be frightened, thinking that it's worse than it is. No, I'd rather say nothing, if you don't mind. I can imagine you frowning at this habit of mine of taking aim and then not firing, of hinting mysteriously, then saying nothing, but at the same time saying something. Well, listen carefully. Ay, ay, ay! Can't you hear your little Beatrice moaning? Do you think these are a lover's complaints, that she is cooing like your doves? No, she is crying out in physical pain. Don't go thinking that I'm a doomed consumptive like *La Dame aux camélias*. No, my love. Don Lope has given me his rheumatism. Now, don't worry, Don Lope can't give me anything anymore...you know what I mean. There's no chance of that, but there is such a thing as accidental contagion. I mean that my tyrant has taken his revenge on my disdain for him by passing on to me, by some gypsy art or evil eye, the devilish illness afflicting him. When I got out of bed two days ago, I felt such a sharp pain, so very sharp. I can't tell you where exactly because, as you know, a young lady, and an English young lady to boot, Miss Restitute, cannot, in the presence of a man, decorously name any parts of her body other than her face and hands. But I trust you, shameless creature that you are, and want to speak openly: My leg hurts. Ay, ay, ay! Do you know where? Just by my knee, where that mole be…Well, if that isn't trust, I don't know what is. Doesn't it seem cruel to you what God is doing to me? It seems only right and proper that He should heap aches and pains upon a rake like him, as punishment for a lifetime of crimes against morality, but why on me, a young thing who has only just begun to sin…and then only in extenuating circumstances? Why punish me so harshly for what is, after all, a first offense? He may be just, but I don't understand it. Aren't we fools? If only we could understand His divine intentions, etc. etc. In short, the Almighty's decrees are causing me terrible suffering. What can it be? Will it go away soon? I despair sometimes and wonder if it isn't God the Almighty who has sent me this ailment but the Prince of Darkness. The Devil is a bad person and wants to avenge himself on me because I angered him. Shortly before I met you, my despair was engaged in negotiating a deal with him, but then I met you and sent him packing. You saved me from falling into his clutches. The wretch swore revenge, and here it is. Ay, ay, ay! Your Restituta, your Curra de Rimini is lame. It's no joke; I can't walk. I'm filled with horror at the idea that, if you were here in Madrid, I wouldn't be able to go to your studio. Although I would, of course, even if I had to drag myself there. Will you still love me as a cripple? You won't make fun of me? You won't lose hope? Tell me that you won't, tell me that this lameness won't last. Come back, I want to see you; it torments me terribly that I can no longer remember your face. I spend long hours of the night trying to imagine what you look like, and I can't. So what do I do? I reconstruct you as best I can, I create you, doing violence to my imagination in the process. Come back soon and, along the way, pray to God, as I do, that when you arrive, your prodigy—or freak—will no longer be lame."

Tuesday

"I bring wonderful news, Señó Juan, man of the country and of country paths, clodhopper, peaceable grower of dates, wonderful news! My leg has stopped hurting! I'm not limping anymore. What relief, what joy! Don Lope is pleased that I'm better, but it seems to me that, in his heart of hearts (that very labyrinthine heart), he is sorry that his slave no longer limps, because lameness is like a shackle that binds her closer to his wretched person. Your letter made me laugh out loud. Seeing my illness as a mere dislocation caused by my attempts to clamber onto the high seat of immortality is really very witty. What troubles me is that you persist in being so stupid and clinging on to such trivial clichés: Life is short and we must enjoy it while we can! Art and glory are not worth a penny! That isn't what you said when we first met, you rascal. That instead of bounding about, I should sit sedately on the warm flagstones of domesticity! I can't! I grow less domestic with each day that passes. The more Saturna tries to teach me, the clumsier I grow. If that is a grave fault, then have pity on me.

"I'm so happy! First, you tell me that you will come and see me soon. Second, I'm no longer lame. Third . . . no, I won't tell you the third thing. Oh, all right, just so that you won't go overexerting your brain, here it is. I couldn't sleep last night, and an idea kept fluttering around me until, finally, it got inside my noodle and made its nest there; and once it had, I was filled with a whole tormenting plague of ideas, which I will reveal to you at once. I have solved the dreaded problem. The sphinx of my destiny opened her marble lips and told me that, in order to be free and honorable, to enjoy full independence and live off my own earnings, I must become an actress. And I agree, I approve, I feel that I *am* an actress. I've never been sure until now that I had the necessary talent to appear on the stage, but now I know that I do. Those talents themselves are inside me, telling me 'Yes!' Feigning emotions and passions, imitating life! What could be easier when I'm capable of feeling not only what I feel now but what I would feel in all kinds of situations. With that, a good voice and a figure that is, shall we say, not too bad, I have all I need.

"I know what you're going to say, that I'll never have the courage to stand up there with all those eyes looking at me, that I'll forget my lines . . . Not at all. Me, embarrassed? I have no shame, in the best possible sense of the word. Right now, I feel ready to play the most difficult and passionate of tragedies and the most delicate, witty, and coquettish of comedies. Are you mocking me? Don't you believe me? Let's try, shall we? Put me on the stage and then you'll see what your Restituta can do. You'll soon be persuaded. What do you think? I imagine you won't like the idea, that you'll feel jealous of the theater. When a young leading man embraces me, or when I have to cuddle up to an actor and speak words of love, that will displease you, won't it? You wouldn't be in the least amused if twenty thousand fools were to fall in love with me and bring me flowers and believe they had the right to declare all kinds of volcanic passions. Don't be silly. I love you more than life itself. But you must at least agree that the dramatic art is a noble art, one of the few that a woman can honorably take up. Please agree, dear fool, and agree, too, that as a profession it would give me independence and that being independent would allow me to love you all the more, especially if you decide to be a major artist. Please do, and don't let me see you transformed instead into an ordinary, obscure landowner. Don't speak to me of obscurity. I want light, more light, always more light."

Saturday

"Ay, ay, ay! All my hopes are dashed. You must have been worried sick, having received no letter from me since Tuesday. Can you guess what has happened to me? I am so unhappy. I'm lame again and in absolute agony! I have spent three dreadful days. I was taken in by that treacherous pseudo-recovery on Tuesday. On Wednesday, after a hellish night, I woke up screaming. Don Lope brought in the doctor, a certain Dr. Miquis, a pleasant young man. How embarrassing! I had no alternative but to show him my leg. He saw the mole, ay, ay ay, and told me all kinds of jokes to make me laugh. His prognosis is not, I think, very hopeful, although Don Lepe assures me that it is, doubtless to cheer me up. How on earth am I ever going to be an actress if I'm lame? It's simply not possible. I'm quite mad. I think only grim thoughts. And what exactly is wrong with me? Nothing really. Near the place where the mole is, there's a hard lump and if I press it or try to walk, I see stars. That Dr. Miquis, damn him, has sent me all kinds of unguents and an endless bandage, which Saturna very, very carefully wraps around my leg. I bet I'm a real picture! Your Beatrice in a poultice! I must look hideous! What a sight! I'm writing to you from an armchair, from which I cannot move. Saturna is holding the inkwell. If you were to come back now, how could I possibly visit you? Don't come until I'm well again. I pray to God and the Virgin that I get better soon. I don't deserve such a punishment, after all, I haven't been so very bad. What crime have I committed? Loving you? Is that a crime? Since I have the dreadful habit of looking for *il perche delle cose*,* I wonder if God has made a mistake, goodness, what blasphemy! No, He doesn't make mistakes. We will suffer. Patience, although, to be frank, not being able to become an actress enrages me and makes me throw away all the patience I had managed to muster. But what if I do get better... because I will, I won't have a limp or only one so slight that I can easily disguise it.

"If you weep not now, when will you ever weep? And if you don't love me more and more and more, you deserve to have the Prince of Darkness take you and put out your eyes. I am so miserable! I don't know whether it's just my distress or the effect of the illness, but it's as if all my ideas had fled, had flown away. Will they ever come back? Do you think they will? Then I start thinking and I say: Dear God, where are all the things I read about, all the things I learned from those big fat books? They must be flitting around my head, the way birds flitter around a tree before roosting for the night, and they will come back, they will. I'm just very sad and low in spirits, and the idea of having to walk on crutches weighs on me. No, I don't want to be lame. I would rather...

"To distract me, Malvina suggested that we start learning German together. I sent her packing. I don't want German, I don't want

---

*"The why of things": a line from Leopardi's poem "Canto Notturno."

languages, all I want is my health back, even if, afterwards, I'm a complete dolt. Will you love me if I'm lame? No, I will get better. Of course I will! It would be so unfair if I didn't, a barbarous act on the part of Providence, of the Almighty, of the...oh, I don't know. I'm going mad. I need to cry, to spend all day crying...but I'm too angry and I can't cry when I'm angry. I hate the whole human race, apart from you. I wish they would hang Malvina, shoot Saturna, publicly whip Don Lope, parade him on a donkey, and then burn him alive. I'm in a terrible state; I don't know what I'm thinking or what I'm saying..."

20

AS EVENING fell on one of the last days in January, a melancholy, taciturn Don Lope Garrido entered his house like a man on whose spirit weighed the very heaviest of griefs and cares. In a matter of a few months, age had invaded the territory that the pride and spirit of his mature years had hitherto always managed to fend off; he was rather stooped now; his noble features had taken on a somber, earthy tinge; the gray hairs on his head were prospering and, to complete this picture of decay, there was also a certain air of neglect about his clothes, which was even more pitiful to see than the deterioration in his physical appearance. His habits had also been affected by this sudden change, for Don Lope now rarely went out at night and spent most of the day at home. One can understand the reason for such a decline because it is worth repeating that, apart from his complete moral blindness in the matter of love, this now redundant libertine was a man of good feelings and could not bear to see the people close to him suffer. True he had dishonored Tristana and ruined her for society and for marriage, trampling her fresh youth, but never confuse kindness with weakness, for he loved her deeply and it pained him immeasurably to see her ill and with little hope of a speedy recovery. According to what Dr. Miquis had said on his first visit, it would be a long process, and he had offered no assurances that she would get well again, that is, recover from her lameness.

Don Lope entered the house and, removing his cape in the hallway, went straight to his slave's room. The poor girl looked so ill from enforced inactivity and from the moral and physical burden of her painful illness! She sat still and quiet in the armchair he had bought for her, and which could be opened out and extended so that she could rest whenever sleep overcame her; wrapped in a checkered shawl, with her hands folded and her head bare, Tristana wasn't a shadow of her former self. Nothing could compare with the pallor of her skin; the paper pulp from which her lovely face seemed to be made was now incredibly diaphanous and white; her lips had taken on a purple tinge; and sadness and continual weeping had encircled her eyes with an opaline transparency.

"How are you, my dear?" Don Lope asked, stroking her cheek and sitting down beside her. "Better, eh? Miquis tells me that you're on the road to recovery and that the pain is a sign that you're improving. It's not a dull pain anymore, is it? It really hurts, doesn't it, the way a bad graze hurts. That's what we want, pain. The swelling's going down. Now, my dear, you must take this," he said, showing her a small box from the pharmacist. "It doesn't taste nasty or anything: just two pills every three hours. As for external medicine, Don Augusto says we should continue as before. So cheer up, in another month or so, you'll be leaping about and even dancing a *malagueña*."

"In another month? I don't think so. You're just saying that to console me. Thank you, but, alas, I won't leap anywhere ever again."

The note of profound sadness in her voice touched Don Lope, who was a brave man, uncowed by other things, but helpless in the face of illness. Seeing a person he loved in physical pain reduced him to being a child again.

"Don't lose hope. I have confidence, and you must as well. Do you need more books to distract you? Do you want to do some drawing? You only have to ask. Shall I bring you some plays so that you can study your parts?" Tristana shook her head. "All right, then, I'll bring you some nice novels or history books. Now that you've started cramming your head with knowledge, you don't want to stop halfway. I have a feeling you're going to be an extraordinary woman. I don't know how I could have been so stupid as not to realize this before. I'll never forgive myself."

"You're forgiven," murmured Tristana, looking deeply bored.

"Shall we eat? Are you peckish? No? Well, you have to make an effort. At least have some soup and a small glass of sherry. What about a chicken leg? No? Well, I won't insist. Now if the illustrious Saturna will give me a little food, I would be most grateful. I'm not that hungry really, but I feel slightly weak and one must feed the inner man."

He went to the dining room, and not even noticing what was in the various dishes, for his thoughts were far removed from external things, he dispatched some soup, a little meat, and so on, then, still chewing the last mouthful, returned to Tristana.

"Now where were we? Did you have some soup? Good. I'm glad you haven't entirely lost your appetite. I'll stay and talk until you fall asleep. No, I'm not going out, I want to keep you company. And I don't say that in order to be thanked. I know there was a time when I should have stayed with you and I didn't. It's late, very late, and these kindnesses of mine are latecomers too. But let's not talk about that; don't make me feel ashamed. If you don't want me here, just say so; if you prefer to be alone, I'll go to my room."

"No, no, stay. When I'm alone, I think dark thoughts."

"Dark thoughts, my dear? What nonsense. You haven't fully grasped the myriad of good things that fate has in store for you. I recognize your qualities, rather late in the day, it's true, but I do recognize them now. And I realize that I am not even worthy of the honor of offering you advice, but I will give the advice anyway and you can take it or leave it, as you wish."

This was not the first time Don Lope had spoken to her in this way; and truth be told, Señorita Reluz listened to him with pleasure, because the smooth-talking gallant knew how to strike the right note, praising her taste and stimulating her dreaming imagination. It should be noted, moreover, that a few days before the scene we have described, the tyrant had given his victim proof of remarkable tolerance. Don Lope had burst in one morning when Tristana was deeply immersed in her epistolary activities, sitting in her chair, resting her letter on the piece of wood that Saturna had prepared for her as a writing tablet. Seeing her hurriedly hiding away both paper and inkwell, he smiled in kindly fashion and said, "No, no, child, you carry on writing your letters. I won't bother you now."

Tristana was astonished to hear these considerate words, which partly gave the lie to the old rogue's jealous, egotistical nature, and so she happily carried on writing. Meanwhile, alone in his room with his conscience, Don Lepe gave himself a good talking-to: "I mustn't make her any more unhappy than she already is. I feel so very sorry for her, the poor love! All right, so recently, feeling alone and bored, she met some good-for-nothing, who turned her head with a few tender words. I don't want to do that nincompoop the honor of worrying about him. Yes, yes, they love each other and have made a thousand foolish promises. Really, young people today have no idea how to win someone's heart, but it would be easy enough to fill with hot air the head of a girl as dreamy and excitable as Tristana. He has doubtless offered to marry her, and she believes him. And of course they exchange little notes and letters. I don't even need to read them to know the kind of nonsense they write. Marriage, marriage, marriage, the usual refrain. Such imbecility would make me laugh if it didn't involve this bewitching child, my last and, therefore, dearest trophy. Good God, to think that I stupidly let her slip away, but I'll get her back, not for any nefarious purposes, of course, I'm not up to that kind of thing anymore, but simply to have the pleasure of snatching her back from that interloper—whoever he is—the man who stole her from me, and to prove that when the great Don Lope's anger is aroused, there isn't a man alive can get the better of him. I will love her like a daughter, I will defend her against all comers, against the various forms and types of love, whether with marriage or without . . . I want to be her father now and keep her to myself, all to myself, because I intend to live for many more years yet, and if she can't be my wife, then I'll have her as my beloved daughter, not that I want anyone else to touch her, mind, or even look at her."

The profound egotism of these ideas was accompanied by a leonine snarl, as usually happened at critical moments in the old gallant's life. He then went immediately to Tristana's side and with a meekness that seemed to come quite naturally to him, he stroked her cheek, saying, "Don't you worry, my poor little love. It is time to bestow a plenary indulgence. I know that you stumbled morally, even before your little leg went lame. No, it's all right, I'm not going to tell you off. It was my fault, yes, mine and mine alone. I must take full blame for your flirtation, which was the result of my neglect and my forgetfulness. You are young and pretty. It's hardly surprising that every young man who sees you flirts with you, or that one of them, slightly better than the others, should have pleased you, and that you should have believed his foolish promises and thrown yourself into plans of happiness that quickly turned to smoke. But let's speak no more of that. I forgive you. Total absolution. You see, I want to be your father now, and I am beginning by..."

Tremulous and fearful lest these words were merely a cunning trick to make her confess her secret, and feeling more than ever under Don Lope's mysterious sway, the captive denied everything, stammering excuses; but the tyrant, with rare affability, redoubled his kind words and fatherly expressions of affection, saying, "There's no point denying what your confusion so clearly declares. I know nothing and I know everything. I know nothing but divine everything. The female heart holds no secrets for me. I have lived. I'm not asking you to tell me who the young gentleman is, because I really don't care. I know the story, it's one of the oldest in the world, one of the most ordinary, common or garden stories in the human repertoire. He will have made you dizzy with the vulgar hope of marriage, suitable only for shop assistants and the lower orders. He will have spoken to you of the altar, the blessings of matrimony, and of a life as coarse as it is obscure, complete with scrap soup, several brats of your own making, knitting while you all sit cozily by the fire in your armchairs, and other such idiocies. And if you swallow the bait, you will be lost, you will ruin your future and give a slap in the face to your destiny—"

"My destiny!" exclaimed Tristana, reviving, her eyes bright.

"Yes, your destiny. You were born for great things, even though, as yet, we do not know what those things are. Matrimony would plunge you back into the common herd. You cannot and must not belong to anyone, only to yourself. Your idea of honorable freedom, devoted to a noble profession—an idea I did not appreciate before, but which has finally won me over—demonstrates the profound logic of your vocation or, if you like, your ambition. And you are worthy of your ambitions. Your will keeps overflowing because your intelligence has burst its banks. There are no two ways about it, my dear child," he went on in a slightly mocking tone. "Fancy talking to a woman like you about such trivialities as scissors and thimbles and egg-laying, fireside chats and a cozy life *à deux*. Be very careful, my child, with these seductions intended for seamstresses and would-be ladies, because your leg *will* get better and you will become the finest actress the world has ever seen. And if the stage doesn't suit you, then you will be something else, whatever you want, whatever you wish to be. I don't know what that will be, neither do you; all we know is that you have wings, but where you will fly to . . . ah, if we knew that, we would penetrate the very mysteries of destiny, and that is forbidden to us."

21

"GOODNESS me," Tristana said to herself, clasping her hands and staring hard at this old man, "the things the rascal knows! He's an out-and-out scoundrel devoid of conscience, but he knows a lot, he really does!"

"Would you agree with me, my dear?" asked Don Lope, kissing her hands, making no attempt to disguise the glee he felt inside as he sensed victory.

"I would have to say 'Yes.' I don't think I am cut out for domesticity, I mean, I just don't see myself in that role . . . But I don't know if the things I dream of will come to anything."

"Oh, I can see it as clear as day!" retorted Don Lope with the honest conviction with which he imbued all his lies. "Believe me, a father is never wrong, and repenting of any harm I ever did, I want to be a father to you now and only a father."

They continued talking about the same subject, and Don Lope, making good use of his strategic skills, managed to capture the enemy position, mockingly describing the banality of an eternal union with some vulgar creature and the tedium of married life.

These ideas both flattered the young woman and served as a palliative for her grave illness. She felt better that evening and, when left alone with Saturna, before the latter went to bed, she experienced moments of elation, her ambitions more keenly felt than ever. "Yes, why shouldn't I become an actress? I will live in decorous freedom, never binding myself eternally to anyone, not even to the man I love and will always love. The freer I am, the more I will love him."

When Saturna, with exquisite care, had attended to her bad knee, replacing the old bandage with a fresh one, she helped Tristana into bed. Tristana spent a restless night, but consoled herself with the effluvia of her overheated imagination and with the thought of her prompt recovery. She waited anxiously for morning so that she could write to Horacio, and at dawn, before Don Lope got up, she launched into a long, excitable epistle.

"My love, my own country bumpkin, *mio diletto*, I am still not well, but I am happy. It's odd, isn't it? I can hardly expect someone else to understand me when I cannot even understand myself! Yes, I am happy and full of hopes that slip into my soul when I least expect them. God is good and sends me these joys, doubtless because I deserve them. I feel that I will get better, and even though I show no signs of doing so, it's enough that I feel it. That allows me to believe I will fulfill my dreams, that I will be an outstanding tragic actress, that I will be able to adore you from the castle of my actorly independence. We will love each other from castle to castle, absolute masters of our respective desires, you will be free and I will be free and yet still your wife, with our own domains, no life in common, no sacred bond, no garlic soup, nothing.

"Don't speak to me of altars, because that makes you shrink before my eyes to such a tiny size that I cannot even see you. Maybe what I'm saying is madness, but I was born to be a chronic madwoman, I'm like a dish of mutton, either take me or leave me. No, don't leave me. I hold on to you, I bind you to me, because my madness needs your love in order to become reason. Without you, I would grow stupid, which is the worst thing that could happen.

"I don't want either of us to be stupid. I enlarge you in my imagination when you try to make yourself small and make you handsome again when you insist on making yourself ugly, abandoning your sublime art in order to cultivate radishes and pumpkins. Don't oppose me in my desires, don't banish my hopes; I want you to be a remarkable man and I intend to have my own way. I can feel it, I can see it … it cannot be otherwise. My inner voice amuses itself by describing to me all the perfections of your being. Don't deny that you are as I dream you to be. Let me fabricate you, no, that's not the word, let me compose you, no, that's not it either, let me reconstruct you, no ... Let me think of you however I want to. That way I am happy: let me, let me ..."

Other letters followed, in which the imagination of the poor patient ran riot in the ideal world, galloping through it like a runaway steed, in search of the impossible end of the infinite, never tiring in its wild, splendid race.

For example:

"How are you, my liege? The more I adore you, the more I forget your physiognomy, but I invent another that is equally to my taste and in accordance with my ideas and the perfections with which I wish to see your sublime person adorned. Shall I tell you a little about myself? I am in terrible pain! I thought I was getting better, but no, for reasons known only to himself, God does not want that. Your beautiful ideal, your Tristanita, may in time be famous, but she will certainly never be a dancer. My leg would not allow it. And for the selfsame reason, I doubt I will ever be an actress. I'm absolutely furious. It gets worse each day. The pain is terrible. What use are doctors? They understand nothing about the art of curing people. I would never have thought that an insignificant thing like a leg could have such influence over a person's destiny, after all, a leg is just for walking on. I always thought it was the brain or the heart that was in charge, but now a stupid knee has turned despot, and those noble organs obey it. Or rather, they don't obey it, they pay it no heed at all, but nevertheless suffer under an absurd despotism, which I trust will be only temporary. It's as if the soldiery had suddenly risen up in revolt, but in the end, the rabble will have to submit.

"And you, my beloved king, how is it with you? If I did not have your love to sustain me, I would already have succumbed to this seditious limb, which wants to have its head. But I will not be cowed, and I continue to think the bold things I have always thought—no, I think more and more such things, and I climb ever upwards. My aspirations are clearer than ever; my ambition, if you can call it that, breaks free and dances like a mad thing. Believe me, you and I are made for greatness. Can you guess how? Well, I can't explain how, but I know it. My heart tells me so and my heart knows everything and has never yet deceived me and cannot deceive me. You yourself do not understand your own worth. Do I need to reveal you to yourself? Look into me, for I am your mirror, and you will see the supreme Mount Tabor of artistic glory. I'm sure you won't laugh at what I say, just as I'm sure that you are exactly as I believe you to be, the summation of moral and physical perfection. There are no defects in you, nor can there be, even though the eyes of the common people may see them. Know yourself; listen to me; surrender yourself without fear to the person who knows you far better than you do. I can't go on. My knee hurts too much. Ah, that a bone, a wretched bone, could . . ."

Thursday

"What a day yesterday was, and what a night! But I will not be cowed. My spirit grows with suffering. Do you know, last night, when that knavish pain gave me a few moments of respite, the knowledge I have acquired from reading, and which had somehow vanished and evaporated, all came back to me. The ideas rushed in one after the other, and memory slammed the door shut so as to keep them in. Don't be surprised; not only do I still know all that I knew, I know more, much more. Other new and unfamiliar ideas joined the old ones. I must be some kind of ideas magnet, which, as it sallies forth into the world, attracts any small ideas it meets and brings them to me. I know more, much more than before. I know everything, well, perhaps not everything. I feel so very relieved today and will devote myself to thinking about you. How good you are! Your intelligence has no equal, your artistic genius knows no bounds. I love you more deeply than ever, because you respect my freedom, because you don't tie me to the leg of a chair or a table with the rope of matrimony. My passion demands freedom. I need a very large field to live in. I need to be free to graze on the grass that will grow all the taller as I crop it from the ground with my teeth. I wasn't made for life in a stable. I need a limitless prairie."

In her later letters, Tristana no longer used the vocabulary with which both had so liberally scattered their intimate conversations, whether spoken or written. She never again referred to Señó Juan or Paca de Rimini, never invented words or took the grammatical liberties that had been the spice of her piquant style. All those things were wiped from her memory, as if Horacio himself were disappearing, to be replaced by an ideal being, the bold creation of her imagination, a being who embodied all the beauties of the world, visible and invisible. Her heart burned with a vast love that one might easily term mystical, given the incorporeal and entirely unreal qualities of the being who provoked such feelings. This new, intangible Horacio bore a slight resemblance to the real one, but only slight. Tristana made of that pretty phantasm the basic truth of her existence, for she lived only for him, not realizing that she was worshipping a God of her own devising. And that worship found expression in sparkling letters, written in a tremulous hand, in between the overwrought states brought on by sleeplessness and fever, letters that she only dispatched to Villajoyosa out of mechanical habit, for they should really have been sent from the post office of daydreams to somewhere out there in imaginary space.

Wednesday

"My lord and master, my pain carries me to you, as would my joys if I had any. Pain and pleasure provoke the same desire to fly... if only one had wings. In the midst of the misfortunes afflicting me, God has been kind enough to give me your love. What does physical pain matter? Not a thing. I will bear it with resignation, as long as you do not hurt me. And let no one say that you are far away! I have you by my side, I sit you down next to me, I see you and touch you; I have enough imaginative power to abolish distance and shrink time at will."

Thursday

"You don't need to tell me, I know that you are as you should be. I can feel it inside. Your peerless intelligence, your artistic genius, send sparks up into my brain. Your lofty sense of goodness seems to have made its nest in my heart. Ah, the power of the spirit! When I think very hard about you, the pain goes. You are my medicine, or at least the anesthetic of which my doctor knows nothing. You should see him. Miquis is astonished at my serenity. He knows I adore you, but he doesn't know your true worth, nor that you are the divinity's choicest fragment. If he did, he would be more sparing in prescribing sedatives, which are far less effective than the thought of you. I have the pain under control at the moment, because I needed a moment's calm in order to write to you. By sheer willpower, of which I have a good deal, and by sheer force of thought, I manage to achieve an occasional respite from pain. Devil take this leg of mine. They can cut it off for all I care. I don't need it. I will love as spiritually with one leg as with two . . . or none at all."

Friday

"I don't have to see your marvelous creations. I can see them as clearly as if they were there before my eyes. Nature holds no secrets for you. She is not so much your teacher as your friend. She slips into your works unasked, and your eyes fix her on the canvas before your brushes do. When I am better, I will do the same. The certainty of what I have to do stirs inside me. We will work together, because I won't be able to be an actress; I see now that it would be impossible. But I could be a painter. I can't get the idea out of my head. A few lessons from you would be enough for me to follow in your footsteps, although always some way behind, of course. Will you teach me? Yes, you will, because your largeness of soul goes hand in hand with your understanding, and, although you won't admit it, you are utter goodness, absolute kindness, supreme beauty."

22

You can imagine the effect on Horacio of these disjointed but subtle thoughts. He found himself transformed into an ideal being, and with each letter that arrived, he was filled with more and more doubts about his own personality, sometimes even going so far as to ask himself if he was as he really was or as painted by the indomitable pen of Don Lepe's visionary little girl. However, his unease and confusion did not prevent him from seeing the danger that lay behind her letters, and he began to think that Paquita de Rimini was perhaps sicker in the head than in her extremities. Assailed by gloomy thoughts and full of anxieties and suspicions, he resolved to travel to Madrid, and had everything ready for the journey at the end of February, when Doña Trinidad suddenly started coughing up blood, and that, alas, kept him tied to Villajoyosa.

At the same time, events of extreme gravity were taking place in Madrid and in Don Lope's house, and these we will describe now. Tristana's condition had deteriorated so much that all her willpower was helpless in the face of the intense pain and fever, vomiting, and general malaise. A desperate and bewildered Don Lope, lacking the presence of mind the situation called for, tried to exorcize the danger by crying out to heaven, at first piteously, then with threats and blasphemies. In his blind fear, he thought a change of treatment would save the patient. Miquis was duly dismissed, only to be recalled because his successor was the kind who cured with leeches, and while this provided some relief at first, it soon demolished Tristana's little remaining strength.

Tristana was cheered by the return of Miquis, because she liked and trusted him, and the therapeutic powers of his sheer affability helped lift her spirits. For a few hours each day, strong sedatives restored to her the precious ability to find consolation in her own imagination, to forget the danger she was in and ponder imaginary hopes and remote glories. She took advantage of those moments to write a few brief, succinct letters, which Don Lope himself would take to the post office, making no mystery now of his indulgent attitude.

"Enough of subterfuge, my dear," he said in confiding, paternal tones. "For me there are no secrets. And if writing your little letters brings you comfort, I will not scold you or try to stop you writing them. No one understands you better than I, and the man lucky enough to read your scribblings is not worthy of them, nor does he deserve such an honor. In time, you will come around to my way of thinking. Meanwhile, my little one, write as much as you wish, and if one day, you are not up to wielding your pen, then you can dictate your words to me, and I will be your secretary. You see how little importance I give to this childish game. For these are childish amusements, which I understand perfectly, because I too was once twenty years old, I too was foolish, and would address every girl I met as *my beautiful ideal* and offer her my pale hand!"

He would conclude these jocular remarks with a somewhat insincere little laugh, in the vain hope that Tristana would laugh with him, but alas, he always laughed alone, all the while hiding the gnawing anxiety inside him.

Augusto Miquis visited her three times a day, yet still this did not satisfy Don Lope, who was determined to use every recourse known to medical science to cure his poor, unhappy "doll." In these circumstances, it wasn't enough for him to give his shirt, his very skin would have seemed too small a sacrifice to achieve such a goal.

"If I run out of money completely," he thought, "which is not impossible at the rate we're going, I will do what I always hated and still hate doing: I will ask for a loan, I will stoop to begging for help from my relatives in Jaén, which for me is the very apogee of humiliation and shame. My dignity is worth nothing in the face of this terrible misfortune tearing at my heart, a heart that was once made of bronze and is now pure butter. Who would have thought it? Nothing touched me then, and the sufferings of all humanity mattered not a jot. But it seems to me now that the leg of this poor young woman could topple the universe. Until this moment, I don't think I realized how much I love her, the poor girl! She is the love of my life, and I will not lose her for all the world. I will do battle for her with God Himself and with death. My egotism could move mountains, I recognize that, but it is an egotism that I would not hesitate to call 'holy,' because it is leading me to a complete reform of my character and of my whole being. It is because of that egotism that I now renounce my scandalous love affairs and pledge to devote myself, if God grants me my wish, to the happiness and well-being of this peerless woman, who is not a woman but an angel of wisdom and grace. I held her in my hands and did not understand who or what she was. Own up, Don Lope, you are an arrant fool, and admit that we only learn by living and that true knowledge grows only in the untilled fields of old age."

In his derangement, he was as prepared to turn to medicine for a solution as to quackery. One morning, Saturna came to him with a story about some charlatan in Tetuán, whose fame and prestige had reached as far as Cuatro Caminos and the very walls of Fuencarral and who was said to be able to cure so-called "white tumors" with the application of what she termed 'erbs. As soon as Don Lope heard of this miracle worker he sent for her, ignoring Don Augusto's disapproving looks. The woman immediately issued a sunny prognosis, declaring that the cure would take a matter of days. Hope stirred in Don Lepe, and he did whatever the old woman told him to. Miquis found out about this that same afternoon but did not get angry, simply making it known that the poultice prescribed by the "good doctor of Tetuán" would do neither harm nor good. Don Lope heaped curses on all quacks living and not yet born, dispatching them to hell in the company of a hundred thousand devils—and scientific method was restored.

Tristana spent a terrible night, with violent attacks of fever interspersed with feelings of intense cold in her back. Utterly downcast, Don Lope had only to see the doctor's face after his usual morning visit to know that the illness was entering a critical phase, for although good Don Augusto was usually able to disguise the truth of his diagnoses in the presence of a patient, on that day, sorrow won out over dissembling. Tristana herself said with apparent calm, "I understand, Doctor. This is the last time. I don't mind. I like death, I'm warming to him. All this suffering is eating away at my will to live. Up until last night, I still thought living was, at least occasionally, a lovely thing, but now I rather think that it might be better to die . . . to feel no pain . . . what a delight that would be!"

Then she burst into tears, and it took all of brave Don Lepe's courage not to weep with her.

Having consoled the patient with a few skillfully invented lies, Miquis shut himself up with Don Lope in the latter's bedroom, leaving his jokes and his mask of easy friendliness at the door, and there he spoke to him in all seriousness.

"Don Lope," he said, placing his hands on the gentleman's shoulders, for the gentleman seemed more dead than alive, "we have reached the point I feared we would reach. Tristana is very gravely ill. To a brave, calm-tempered man like yourself, capable of accommodating yourself to the most painful circumstances in life, I feel I must speak clearly."

"Yes," murmured Don Lope, putting on a brave face, meanwhile feeling as if the sky were falling in on him, which is why he instinctively raised his hands to hold it up.

"A very high fever and cold in the base of the spine can mean only one thing, as you know, don't you? It's an unmistakable symptom of reabsorption . . . of blood-poisoning, sepsis."

"Yes, and—"

"There's no alternative, my friend. Be brave now. We have to operate."

"Operate!" cried Don Lope, utterly stunned. "You mean cut it off? And you think—"

"It could save her life, although I can't be sure."

"But when?"

"Today. There's no time to lose. An hour's delay and we might be too late."

Don Lope was gripped by a kind of madness when he heard this and began lurching around like a wounded animal, bumping into the furniture and striking himself on the head. Finally, he uttered this incoherent, unconnected stream of words: "Poor child! Cut off her leg... Mutilate her horribly... And what a leg, Doctor! One of Nature's masterpieces. Phidias himself would have wanted it to make his immortal statues. But what kind of science is it that can only cure by cutting? You haven't a clue, you doctors. Please, Don Augusto, for your own soul's sake, think of some other remedy. Cut off her leg! If I could make her better by having myself cut in half, I would do it—right now. Yes, cut off her leg... and don't bother with the chloroform."

The good gentleman's cries must have been audible in Tristana's room, because Saturna rushed in, looking very frightened, to ask whatever had come over her master.

"Get out of here, you mischief-maker. It's all your fault. I mean, no... Oh, I don't know what to think. Off you go, Saturna, and tell the child I won't let them cut off so much as a sliver of her leg. I'd rather cut off my own head. No, don't tell her that. Say nothing. That way she won't know, except she'll have to be told. I'll do it. Be very careful what you say, Saturna. Now go, leave us."

And turning to the doctor, he said, "Forgive me, my dear Augusto. I don't know what I'm saying. I'm quite mad. We will do whatever the doctors decide. What do you think? Must it be today?"

"Yes, the sooner the better. My friend, Dr. Ruiz Alonso, a leading surgeon, will come and... well, we'll see. I believe that if the amputation goes well, she has a good chance of surviving."

"A good chance! So it's still not sure... Ah, doctor, don't think the worse of me for being such a coward. I'm no use in these situations. I revert to being a boy of ten. Who would have thought it! I, who have faced far worse dangers without so much as batting an eyelid."

"Don Lope," said Miquis sadly, "it is on these testing occasions that we discover just how well we will cope with misfortune. Many who consider themselves cowards turn out to be brave, and others who thought they were cock of the walk turn out to be mere chickens. You'll cope."

"We'll have to prepare her. Oh dear God, what a tragedy! I can't do it, Don Augusto, I'm not strong enough."

"Poor child! We won't tell her directly. We'll deceive her."

"Deceive her! You haven't yet realized how keen-eyed she is."

"Well, let's go then and just hope for some unexpected, favorable turn of events. If she's as sharp-witted as you believe, it may be that she has realized already and then we won't need to say anything... The patient often sees things very clearly."

23

THAT WISE student of Hippocrates was quite right. When they went in to see Tristana, she greeted them with a look that was part smiling, part tearful. She laughed, and two large tears ran down her paper cheeks.

"It's all right, I know what you're going to say. There's no need to be upset. I'm brave. I feel almost glad, almost without... because it's best if they cut it off. That way I won't suffer anymore. And what does it matter if I do have only one leg, given that I don't really have two legs as it is, since this one is of no use anyway. Cut it off and then I'll get better and be able to walk again, with crutches or however God teaches me."

"You'll be absolutely fine, my dear," said Don Lope, emboldened by her cheerful mood. "If I thought that cutting off both my legs would free me from my rheumatism, I wouldn't hesitate. After all, legs can be replaced by mechanical devices made by the English and the Germans, and you can walk better on them than on the two wretched oars with which Nature has fitted us."

"Anyway," added Miquis, "there's no need for you to be afraid, you won't feel a thing. You won't even know it's happened. And then you'll be well again and in a few days' time you can get back to your painting."

"Or even today," said old Don Lope, screwing up his courage and trying to swallow down the knot in his throat. "I'll bring you your easel and your paint box, and you'll paint us some really lovely pictures."

Augusto took his leave with a cordial handshake, saying that he would be back soon, although without specifying an exact time, and when Tristana and Don Lope were left alone, they sat for a while in silence.

"I must write a letter," said the patient.

"Do you think you can, my dear? You're very weak. Dictate it to me, and I'll write it."

As he said this, he brought over the piece of wood that served as a writing tablet, along with the paper and inkpot.

"No, I can write. It's very strange what's happening to me now. My leg doesn't hurt anymore. I can barely feel it at all. Of course I can write. My hand is a little shaky, but I can manage."

In the presence of her tyrant, she wrote these lines:

"I'm not sure if the news I am sending is good or bad. They are going to cut off my leg, my poor little leg! But it's my leg's fault. Why is it misbehaving like this? I don't know whether to be glad or not, because my leg is of no use to me as it is. I don't know whether to feel sad, because they are, after all, removing part of my person ... and my body will be different from the one I've had up until now. What do you think? Why get so upset over a leg? You, who are all spirit, will see it like that. I do. And you will love me just as much with one oar as with two. Now I realize it would have been a mistake to devote myself to the stage. A most ignoble art, one that wearies the body and jades the soul. Painting, though, is quite another matter. They tell me I will feel no pain when they ... shall I say the word? ... when they operate. To be frank, it's all very sad, and the only thing that makes it bearable is knowing that, as far as you're concerned, I will be the exactly the same person after they have butchered me. Do you remember that cricket we had, which sang more and better after it lost one of its legs? I know you well, and I know that you will value me no less. You don't need to reassure me on that score. So why, then, am I not happy? It will mean an end to my suffering. God gives me strength and tells me that I will survive this and once again enjoy health and happiness, and be able to love you as much as I wish, and be a painter or a sage and a philosopher. But, no, I can't be happy. I want to cheer myself up, but I can't. That's enough for today. I know you will always love me, but tell me that it's so anyway. Since you cannot deceive me, and since there is no room for lies in a being who embodies every form of goodness, what you say will be my gospel. If you had neither arms nor legs, I would love you just as much, therefore..."

So tremulous was her writing that the last lines were barely legible. When she put down her pen, the poor, unhappy doll fell into deep despair. She wanted to tear the letter up, regretting having written it, but instead handed it, unfolded, to Don Lope, so that he could put it in an envelope and send it to its addressee. This was the first time she had made no attempt to conceal her secret correspondence. Don Lope took it to his room and read it slowly, surprised at the serenity with which Tristana wrote of such a grave matter.

"Now," he said, as he wrote the address on the envelope and as if he were speaking to the person whose name he was writing, "I do not fear you in the least. You have lost her, you have lost her forever, because all that stuff and nonsense about eternal love, ideal love, without legs or arms, amounts to nothing but the ardent ravings of the imagination. I have beaten you. It is a sad but certain victory. God knows I cannot rejoice in that, unless I were to remove the reason for it, which is the greatest sorrow of my life. She belongs to me now, absolutely, and until the end of my days. Poor wingless doll! She tried to escape me, she tried to fly, but reckoned without her fate, which allows her no flutterings, no flittings; she reckoned without God, who is devoted to me—although quite why I have no idea—and brings her to me, bound hand and foot. Poor dear love, my adorable girl, I love her and will always love her—like a father. No one will take her away from me, not now."

At the bottom of those sad feelings, which Don Lope kept locked in his heart, there beat a kind of pride, an elemental, very human egotism of which he himself was unaware. "Mine forever! She will never escape me now!" In repeating that idea to himself, he seemed to be trying to postpone the contentment it brought him, for it was hardly the right moment to feel glad about anything.

He went back into the room to find a very downcast Tristana, and in order to cheer her up, he deployed both pious arguments and ingenious explanations as to why our lower limbs are really utterly useless. Tristana was persuaded, reluctantly, to take some food; Don Lope himself could eat nothing. At two o'clock, Miquis, Ruiz Alonso, and a medical student who would act as assistant all arrived and filed silently and gravely into the living room. One of them was carrying the case containing the tools of the trade, discreetly wrapped in a piece of cloth. Shortly afterwards, in came a boy carrying the bottles of liquid antiseptics. Don Lope received them as one might an executioner on his way to ask the condemned man's forgiveness and prepare him for the execution.

"Gentlemen," he said, "this is a very sad business, very sad..."

And he could utter not another word more. Miquis went into the patient's room and announced blithely, "Fair maiden, we are not all yet come... or, rather, I have come alone. Now let's see how that pulse of yours is doing..."

Tristana turned deathly pale, fixing the doctor with a look that was at once fearful, childish, and pleading. To soothe her, Miquis assured her that he was confident of a complete and radical cure, that her excited state was merely the precursor to a clear and indubitable improvement, and that to calm her down, he was going to give her a little ether.

"It's nothing, my dear, I just put a few drops of liquid on a handkerchief, let you breathe it in, and those rascally nerves will soon fall into line..."

She was not easy to deceive however. The poor young woman knew what his intentions were and, trying very hard to smile, she said, "You want to send me to sleep, don't you? Fine. I look forward to experiencing that deep sleep, in the face of which all pain, however obstinate, is helpless. How nice. And what if I don't wake up, what if I stay there?"

"What do you mean 'stay there'? That would make us look very foolish," said Augusto, just as Don Lope entered looking half dead with worry.

And turning their backs on the patient, they set about preparing the drug, placing on a sideboard the small bottle of precious anesthetic. The doctor made a little nest of his handkerchief and in it placed the balls of cotton wool impregnated with chloroform, and the room filled up with a strong smell of apples.

"What a lovely smell!" said Tristana, closing her eyes, as if in silent prayer.

And Augusto immediately placed the handkerchief over her nose. An initial somnolence was succeeded by anxiety, an epileptic restlessness, convulsions, and uncontrollable, incomprehensible chatter, rather as if she were drunk.

"I don't want it, I don't ... It doesn't hurt anymore. Why cut it off? There I was playing one of Beethoven's sonatas and playing it really well, sitting at the piano, when one of those rude fellows comes along and pinches me on the leg! Let them slice away, let them cut it off ... and I'll keep on playing. The piano holds no secrets for me ... I am Beethoven, his heart, his body, although my hands are my own. Don't let them take my hands from me too, because then ... I won't let them have this hand; I'll hold on to it with the other one so that they can't take it ... and hold on to the other one with this, that way they won't be able to take either of them. You're no gentleman, Miquis, you never have been, you don't even know how to treat a lady, still less an eminent artist ... I wouldn't want Horacio to come and see me like this. He'll get the wrong idea. If Señó Juan was here, he would never allow such a crime to be committed ... Tying up a poor woman and placing such a big stone on her chest, so big ... and then filling up her palette with ashes so that she can't paint ... How extraordinary! How strong they smell, these flowers I painted! I painted them, so how is it that now they are alive? The power of artistic genius! I'll have to retouch that Velázquez painting of *The Spinners* and see if I can improve it. Perfection, devilish perfection, where are you? Saturna, Saturna ... come quickly, I'm suffocating. The perfume from those flowers ... No, no, it's the painting that smells, the prettier the flowers, the more poisonous ..."

At last she was still, her mouth half open, her pupils motionless. Now and then, she would utter a childish moan, a timid protest from the person crushed beneath the stone slab of that brutal sleep. Before the chloroforming was done, two more executioners, for that was how Don Lope thought of them, came into the room, and as soon as they felt the patient was ready, they placed her on a bed covered by a mat made for the purpose and, without losing a second, they set about their sad labors. Don Lope gritted his teeth, and every now and then, unable to bear the pitiful scene, he would go off to his own room only to return at once, ashamed of his cowardice. He saw them apply the Esmarch bandage—a piece of rubber resembling a snake. Then they began cutting into the chosen incision point; and when they pared away the flap of skin that would be used later on to make the stump, when Don Lope saw the first blood spilled as the diligent scalpel sliced in, his cowardice became proud, stoical, unbending valor. His heart turned once more to bronze, his face to parchment, and he remained valiantly present until the end of that cruel operation, carried out with consummate skill and swiftness by the three doctors. An hour and a half after the chloroform was administered, Saturna rushed from the room carrying a long, narrow object wrapped in a sheet. Shortly afterwards, with the arteries ligatured, the skin sewn onto the stump, and after the painstaking, careful application of antiseptic, Señorita Reluz began her slow, sad awakening, her new life, her resurrection after that simulacrum of death, leaving her foot and two-thirds of her leg in the depths of that apple-scented tomb.

24

"Ah, it still hurts!" Those were the first words she spoke when she returned from the dark abyss. And then her pale, distraught features revealed a profound process of self-analysis, similar to the intense effort of observation that the fearful direct toward their own organs, listening to their breathing and the flow of their blood, mentally feeling their muscles, and eavesdropping on every tremor of their nerves. The poor girl was doubtless focusing all her mental energies on the empty space where her leg had been, in order to replace the lost limb and restore it to how it was before the illness, healthy and vigorous and agile. It was easy enough to imagine that she still had both her legs and was walking elegantly along with the quick, light pace that would carry her in a trice to Horacio's studio.

"How are you, my child?" asked Don Lope, stroking her.

And touching the white hair of that faded gallant, she answered playfully, "Very well. I feel quite rested. If you let me, I would break into a run right now...well, perhaps not a run. That wouldn't be a good idea."

When the others had left, Augusto and Don Lope assured her that the cure would be complete and congratulated themselves on a surgical success with an enthusiasm they quite failed to communicate to her. They lifted her carefully onto her bed, with an eye to both comfort and hygiene, and then there was nothing more to be done but wait for the next ten or fifteen critical days.

During that time, Don Lope did not have a moment's peace, because although the wound seemed to be healing well, Tristana sank into an alarming state of dejection and prostration. She did not seem at all the same person, as if she were repudiating her old self; not once did she think of writing a letter or speak of the sublime aspirations or desires that rose up in her ever restless and ambitious spirit; nor did she come out with witty comments and jokes as she had even during the cruelest hours of her illness. Made glum and dull, her brilliant talent suffered a total eclipse. At first, Don Lope enjoyed this new passivity and meekness but soon came to regret her change of character. Like a solicitous father, he never left her side, his fondness and affection sometimes bordering on the cloying. Finally, on the tenth day, Miquis declared that the healing process was progressing precisely as he had hoped and that the invalid would soon be up and about. This coincided with a sudden resurrection of her spirits and, one morning, displeased with herself, she said to Don Lope, "Goodness, I haven't written a letter in days. How rude of me!"

"'There's no hurry, my child," the old gallant replied drily. "No ideal and perfect being would be annoyed simply because he hadn't received a letter; he would console himself for being forgotten by strolling, undaunted, about the ethereal regions in which he lives. But if you want to write, here are your tools. I'll be your secretary. You can dictate your letter to me."

"No, I'll write it myself. Or, if you like, you could write. Just a few words."

"Right, start dictating," said Don Lope, pen in hand and paper at the ready.

"As I was telling you," said Tristana, "I have only one leg now. I'm better though. It doesn't hurt anymore ... I suffer very little ... That will do."

"Aren't you going to continue?"

"I'd best write it myself. I can't think when I'm dictating."

"Here you are, then. You write what you like." And he gave her the pen and set before her the tray with the blotter and the writing paper. "What? Nothing to say? Where has all that inspiration gone, all those bright ideas?"

"I'm so dull. My head's completely empty."

"Shall I dictate to you, then? How about this: 'How handsome you are and what a rascal God made you and how... *unpleasant* such perfection is! No, I won't marry you or any other terrestrial or celestial seraph...' What are you laughing at? Come on. 'I will not marry... Lame or not, that is none of your business. I have someone who loves me just as I am now, and for whom I am worth more with one leg than I was before with two. For your information, I should also tell you that I have since sprouted wings. My papa is going to bring me all the implements I need in order to paint, what's more, he will buy me an organ and find me a teacher so that I can learn to play good music. You'll see, compared to me, the angels of heaven will seem mere buskers.'"

They both burst out laughing and, cheered by his success, Don Lope continued harping on the same theme, until Tristana had to bring the conversation to an abrupt close, saying very seriously, "No, really, I'll write to him... on my own."

Don Lope left her alone for a moment, and Tristana wrote her letter, which was brief and heartfelt.

"Lord of my soul: Tristana is not what she was. Will you still love me just as much? My heart tells me that you will. You seem so much farther off to me than you ever did before, more beautiful, more inspired, more generous, more considerate. Can I come to you with the wooden leg I think they will give me? Won't I look lovely! Goodbye. Don't come and see me. I will adore you from afar, I will raise you up in your absence. You are my God and, like God, invisible. Your very grandeur removes you from my sight... although with the eyes of my soul I can see you clearly enough. Goodbye for now."

She herself sealed the letter and stuck on the stamp before handing the envelope to Saturna, who smiled slightly mockingly as she took it. In the afternoon, when they were alone for a moment, the maid spoke openly.

"I didn't want to say anything this morning because Don Lepe was with you. I didn't send the letter. After all, why put it in the post when Don Horacio is here in Madrid? I'll deliver it to him personally this evening."

When she heard this, Tristana turned first white and then scarlet. She didn't know what to say; not a thought came into her mind.

"You're mistaken," she said at last. "You must have seen someone who looks like him."

"How could I possibly not know him! What an idea! It was him. We talked for more than half an hour. He was determined that I should tell him everything, point by point. You should have seen him, miss! He's as black as my shoe. He says he's been spending all his time either up in the hills or down by the sea, and that it's really beautiful there, really lovely. Anyway, I told him everything, and the poor man, because he loves you so much, didn't take his eyes off me for a minute all the while I was talking. He's says he'll speak to Don Lope and put things straight with him."

"Put what straight?"

"He'll know what to say. He's dying to see you. We'll have to arrange it when the master goes out..."

Tristana said nothing. A moment later, she asked Saturna to bring her a mirror and when she saw herself in it, she grew extremely distressed.

"You're not so very disfigured," said Saturna.

"Oh, please, I look like death. Awful..." And she burst into tears. "He won't recognize me. My skin is the color of brown paper! And how big my eyes have grown. And that mouth! Saturna, take the mirror away and don't give it back to me even if I ask you to."

Contrary to his own desires, which would have kept him tied to the house, Don Lope was often obliged to leave, driven by necessity, which, in those sad circumstances, filled his existence with bitterness and anxiety. The vast expense incurred by the young woman's illness had eaten up the miserable remnants of his already exhausted fortune, and there were days, alas, when the noble gentleman had to do violence to his own sensibilities and go entirely against his nature, knocking at the door of some friend with requests that seemed to him utterly ignominious. How the unhappy gentleman suffered is beyond description. In a matter of a few days, he aged five years. "Who would have thought it... good God, me, Lope Garrido, having to descend to...Me, with my pride and my punctiliousness about safeguarding my dignity, lowering myself to ask certain favors! And the day will come when insolvency will oblige me to ask for money I will not be able to repay...God knows I only bear such shame and degradation in order to sustain my poor girl and bring her joy. Otherwise, I would put a bullet through my brain and be done with it, dispatching my soul to the next world and my weary bones to the grave. Death before shame...But circumstances dictate the very opposite—a life stripped of dignity. I would never have believed it. And then people say that character...but I don't believe in character. There are only facts, accidents. The lives of others provide the mold for our own life and the pattern for our actions."

In Tristana's presence, poor Don Lepe concealed these terrible woes, and even allowed himself to pretend that his situation could not have been more flourishing. He not only bought her the equipment she needed for her painting (two paint boxes—one for oils and the other for watercolors—brushes, easels, and the rest); he also bought her the organ and harmonium he had promised, so that she could amuse herself with music when her painting permitted. Tristana had received sufficient piano tuition at school to be able to fumble her way through some polkas and waltzes and a few other easy pieces. It was a little late now to acquire the kind of skill that only early application and hard work can bring; however, with a good teacher, she could overcome certain difficulties, and besides, the organ did not require such rapid finger work. She was more excited about music than about painting and longed to be able to get out of bed and try her skills. She would learn to manage the pedals with just one foot. While she waited with feverish impatience for the teacher announced by Don Lope, she could hear in her head the instrument's sweet harmonies, albeit less lovely and heartfelt than those playing in the depths of her soul. She believed that she was called to become a remarkable performer, a concert artist of the first order, and this idea cheered her and gave her many hours of happiness. Garrido took pains to encourage that ambitious hope and, meanwhile, reminded her of her earlier attempts at drawing, urging her to put brush to canvas or board and reproduce some lovely subject copied from nature.

"Come on, why don't you start with a portrait of me or of Saturna?"

The invalid replied that she would prefer to train her hand with a little copying, and Don Lope promised to bring her some fine studies of heads or landscapes so that she could choose.

The poor gentleman was prepared to make any sacrifice in order to please his poor little lame girl and—such are the caprices of fickle fate!—when he had no idea where to find such pictorial studies, chance or the devil, in the shape of Saturna, solved the problem.

"But sir," said Saturna, "I know where to find them. Don't be stubborn now. Leave it to me and I'll..."

And with her admirably expressive eyes and gestures, she completed her bold thought.

"Do as you wish, woman," said Don Lope, with shrug. "As far as I'm concerned..."

Half an hour later, Saturna returned from the street with a pile of painted panels and stretchers, heads, naked torsos, sketches of landscapes, still lifes, fruits and flowers, all the work of a master's hand.

25

THESE paintings made a deep impression on Señorita Reluz, like friendly faces seen again after a long absence, reminding her of happier times. Once, they had been for her like living people, and she did not need to strain her imagination overmuch to see them spring into life, moving their lips and fixing her with affectionate eyes. She ordered Saturna to arrange the canvases around her room so that she could enjoy looking at them, and she was transported back to the delicious afternoons she had spent with Horacio in his studio. She grew sad, however, when she compared her present with that past, and in the end begged Saturna to put them away until she could accustom herself to looking at them with less emotion; yet she appeared unsurprised that the paintings should have traveled from studio to house nor did she express any curiosity as to what the suspicious Don Lope thought about it. Saturna did not want to explain nor was she asked to and, shortly afterwards, at about midday, while she was serving the master his miserable lunch of potatoes and a morsel of meat claiming to be a cutlet, she ventured to tell him a few home truths, safe in the trust she inspired after her long service to the household.

"Señorita Tristana's friend wishes to see her, sir, as is only natural. Don't be unkind now and bear in mind the circumstances. They are young, and you are better fitted now to be a father or grandfather than anything else. Aren't you always saying what a big heart you have?"

"Saturna," retorted Don Lope, striking the table with the handle of his knife, "I have the biggest heart in the world, bigger than this house, bigger than the water tower over there."

"Well, then...let bygones be bygones! You're not young any-more, thank God, I mean, unfortunately. Don't be a dog in the man-ger. If you want God to forgive you all your mischief and naughti-ness, all those deceived wives and husbands, just remember that the young are young, and that the world and life and all the good things in it are for those who are just beginning to live, not for those near the end...And so, Don Lepe, I mean, Don Lope, could you not make a—how can I put it—make a gesture..."

Instead of getting angry, the poor gentleman took it as a joke.

"A gesture, eh? And what makes you think I'm so very old? Do you think I'm completely useless? There are those who would be per-fectly happy, yourself included, even at fifty—"

"Fifty? Don't egzaggerate, sir."

"All right, thirty...five."

"Thirty-two and not a year more!"

"As you wish, but if I were of a mind and you...no, don't blush. Anyone would think you were a gargoyle! If you cleaned yourself up a bit, you'd be quite presentable. Why, your eyes alone—"

"Sir, please, you're surely not going to start flirting with *me*, are you?" said Saturna, not hesitating to place the empty dish of meat on one side of the table and sit down opposite her master, arms akimbo.

"No, you're right, I'm in no state to cause any mischief now. You need fear nothing from me. I've hung up my spurs and that's an end to my pranks and my evil ways. I love Tristana so much that the other love I bore her has, quite naturally, turned into fatherly love, and to make her happy, I'm capable of all kinds of gestures, as you put it. So what about this good-for-nothing, then?"

"For heaven's sake, don't call him that. Don't be so proud. He's very handsome."

"And what would you know about handsome men?"

"Sir, that's something all women know about. And while com-parisons may be odorous, I would say Don Horacio's a very good-looking lad...not to be compared with you, of course. Everyone knows that you were the be-all and end-all of handsome men, but that's over now. Look in the mirror and you'll see that you're certainly not handsome anymore. All you have to do is to recognize that Don Horacio—"

"I've never even seen the lad, but I don't need to see him to tell you that nowadays there are no proud, bold, handsome men capable of winning a woman's love. That race of men is extinct. But anyway, let's take it as read that the dauber is relatively handsome."

"Señorita Tristana loves him. Now don't get angry, the truth first and foremost. And youth is youth."

"All right, so she loves him, but I can tell you now: That boy won't make her happy."

"He says he doesn't care that she's lame."

"Saturna, how little you understand of human nature. I'm telling you: That young man will not make Tristana happy. I know about these things. And I'll tell you something else: Tristana doesn't expect to be made happy by that man—"

"Sir!"

"In order to understand these matters, Saturna, it is necessary to, well, understand them. You are not intelligent enough to see beyond the end of your nose. Tristana, believe it or not, *is* a woman of understanding and ardent imagination. She is in love—"

"I know that much."

"No, you don't. She is in love with a man who does not exist, because he doesn't, Saturna; if he did, he would be God, and God doesn't bother coming down to earth in order to amuse young girls. Anyway, that's enough chitchat. Bring me my coffee."

Saturna ran into the kitchen and, when she returned with the coffee, made bold to comment on Don Lope's last remarks.

"Sir, all I'm saying is that, for good or ill, they love each other, and Don Horacio wants to see her. His intentions are honorable."

"Let him come then. His departure will be equally honorable, I'm sure."

"What a tyrant you are!"

"I'm no tyrant. I won't stop them seeing each other," said the gentleman, lighting a cigarette. "But I must speak to him first. You see how kind I am. You said you wanted a gesture. Yes, I will speak to him and tell him...well, what I tell him is up to me."

"You'll probably try and scare him off, I bet."

"No, I myself will bring him to her. That, Saturna, is what I call a gesture. Please inform him that I will visit him in his studio one afternoon this week...tomorrow, in fact. I've made up my mind," he said, pacing restlessly up and down the dining room. "If Tristana wishes to see him, I will not deprive her of that pleasure. Whatever the child wants, her loving father will give her. I bought her paintbrushes, I bought her a harmonium, but that was not enough. She needs more toys. So let him come, her hope, her illusion. Tell me now, Saturna, that I am not a hero, a saint. With that one gesture I wash away all my guilt and deserve God to clasp me to Him as one of His own. So—"

"I'll tell him. But no tricks, eh? If you try and frighten the poor boy—"

"Just seeing me will be enough to frighten him, Saturna, I am what I am...Oh, and another thing: prepare Tristana. Tell her that I will turn a blind eye, that I will leave the house one afternoon so that he can visit and they may talk for half an hour, no more...My dignity will permit no more than that. But I will, in fact, remain in the house, and you and I will open the door just a crack so that we can see how they behave and what they say."

"Sir!"

"It's not your business. Do as I tell you."

"Well, do as I advise then. There's no time to lose. Don Horacio is in a hurry."

"In a hurry? There speaks a young man. In that case, I will visit his studio this very afternoon. Tell him. Off you go. And afterwards, when you join your mistress, you may mention the matter to her, tell her that I neither consent to nor will I oppose the visit...rather, I tolerate it and am prepared to look the other way. And don't let her know that I am going to the studio, because such an act, so out of character, might lower me in her esteem...although perhaps it wouldn't... Anyway, prepare her so that she is not too overcome when she finds herself in the presence of that ideal beauty."

"Don't mock."

"I'm not. By 'ideal beauty' I merely mean—"

"Her type... her kind of man, I suppose."

"Well, you may suppose all you like," he said with a laugh. "Enough talk. You prepare her for the meeting while I go and meet the young gallant."

At the agreed hour—Saturna having warned Don Horacio in advance—Don Lope went to the studio, and as he climbed somewhat wearily up the interminable staircase, he was thinking, as he coughed and wheezed his way upwards, "What very strange things I've been obliged to do lately! Sometimes I feel like asking myself: Are you really Don Lope? I never thought I would reach the stage where I didn't even resemble myself. I will try not to frighten the innocent boy too much."

That first encounter was somewhat strained, neither man knowing quite what attitude to take, torn between benevolence and what one might call a decorative dignity. The painter was prepared to treat Don Lope as Don Lope treated him. And after the usual greetings and compliments, the older gallant behaved toward him with a somewhat disdainful courtesy, treating the young man as if he were an inferior being, whom he was honoring with this brief meeting, imposed on him by chance.

"You know, of course, about the misfortune that has befallen the child. Terrible, isn't it? And she had such talent, such grace! Her life has been quite ruined. You will understand my grief. I look on her as a daughter and love her deeply, with the most pure and disinterested of affections, and since I was unable to preserve her health or save her from that vile amputation, I wish to bring her a little cheer, to make her life more pleasant, insofar as that is possible, and to divert her mind. In short, her unpredictable spirit needs toys. Painting is not enough to distract her, although music may... Her tireless enthusiasms demand more, always more. I happen to know that you—"

"So you consider me a toy, Don Lope," said Horacio with polite good humor.

"No, not a toy exactly, but ... as you can see, I am old, but I have vast experience of life's passions and affections, and I know that youthful inclinations always do have something of the nursery about them. Don't be offended, please. We perceive things differently depending on our age. The prism through which we look when we are twenty-five or thirty distorts things in the most charming way, so that we see them in a fresh, new light. The lens I look through now shows things quite differently. In a word: I view Tristana's inclination with fatherly indulgence, the indulgence with which I would treat any ailing creature, whose every whim and fancy, however extravagant, must be met."

"Forgive me, sir," said Horacio gravely, resisting the fascination of the other gentleman's penetrating gaze, which was slowly sapping his courage, "but I cannot see Tristana's 'inclination' for me, still less my inclination for her, from the point of view of a doting grandfather."

"Well, let's not argue about that," answered Garrido, exaggerating his urbane and scornful tone. "My thoughts are such as I have laid before you; you may think as you wish. Later on, who knows, you may change your mind. I am too long in both tooth and experience to change mine. Anyway, I leave you free to think as you wish. I have come to tell you that since you want to see Tristanita and since Tristanita would be happy to see you, I will not oppose your honoring my house with your presence; on the contrary, I would be most pleased. Did you perhaps imagine that I was going to play the jealous father or the domestic tyrant? No, I dislike deceit of any kind, still less when it comes to something as innocent as your visit. It would be most indecorous for Tristana's sweetheart to try and slip into the house behind my back. Neither of us would gain anything by that, either you sidling in without my permission or me bolting the door as if against some mischief. So, Don Horacio, you may visit Tristana—at an hour of my choosing, of course. And should it prove necessary for you to visit her again, always assuming that your visits bring consolation to my patient, you must promise me never to enter my house without my knowledge."

"That seems most reasonable," said Horacio, who was gradually being won over by the elegant old man's sharp mind and worldly wisdom. "I am entirely at your disposal."

Horacio was conscious of his interlocutor's superiority and felt almost—no, there was no "almost" about it, he felt genuinely pleased to meet him and to admire, for the first time, this curious example of a highly developed social fauna, a legendary, almost poetic figure. This attraction only grew with Don Lope's extremely witty comments on the life of the gallant, on women, and on matrimony. In short, Horacio liked him, and the two men parted with Horacio promising to obey Don Lope's orders and to visit the poor invalid the following afternoon.

26

"A VERITABLE angel!" thought Don Lope as he descended the stairs from the studio, feeling rather less assured than he had on the way up. "And he seems so honest and decent. He doesn't appear to be so very bound to that childish mania for marriage, and he never once mentioned 'the beautiful ideal,' or anything about loving her until death did them part, with leg or without it. No, that's all over... Here I was expecting to meet a romantic, with the face of one who had tasted the vinegar of frustrated passion, and instead I find a healthy young man with a good color and a serene mind, a sensible fellow, who will, in the end, see matters as I do. One wouldn't think that he was so very much in love as, one assumes, he must have been once. Rather, he seems confused, as if he didn't quite know how he should react when he sees her or how to present himself. What will come of all this? For my part, I think it's over and done with, dead and buried, like Tristana's leg."

The marvelous prospect of Horacio's imminent visit troubled Tristana, who, while appearing to believe everything she was told, could not, deep down, quite accept the reality of that visit, for in the days preceding her operation she had grown accustomed to the idea that her beautiful ideal was no longer there; and his very beauty and his rare perfection presented themselves in her mind as things that would shrivel and vanish with proximity. At the same time, a purely human and selfish desire to see and hear the object of her desires struggled in her soul with that unbridled idealism, which, far from seeking proximity, tended, without her realizing it, to avoid it. Distance had come to be one of the most voluptuous aspects of that subtle love striving to detach itself from all sensory influence.

It was while she was in this state of mind that the hour of their interview arrived. Don Lope pretended to absent himself without making any reference to the meeting; instead, though, he stayed in his room ready to emerge should anything happen that might require his presence. Tristana arranged her hair as she had in happier times, and having recovered somewhat during the past few days, she looked very well. She, however, put down the mirror, feeling dissatisfied and anxious, for her idealism did not preclude vanity. When she heard Horacio arrive—Saturna having ushered him into the drawing room—Tristana grew pale and felt almost as if she were about to faint. The little blood in her veins rushed to her heart; she could barely breathe, overwhelmed by a curiosity stronger by far than any other feeling. "Now," she said to herself, "I will find out what he is like, I will see his face, which was long ago erased, forcing me to invent another for my own personal use."

Finally, Horacio came in. At first, to Tristana's surprise, he seemed like a stranger. He walked straight over to her with open arms and tenderly caressed her. For some time, neither of them could speak. Tristana was surprised, too, by the timbre of her former lover's voice, as if she had never heard it before. And then, what a face, what skin, so bronzed by the sun!

"How you've suffered, my poor love!" Horacio said, when sheer emotion allowed him to speak clearly. "And I could not be by your side! It would have been such a solace to me to be able to accompany my Paquilla de Rimini throughout that torment, to keep her spirits up . . . but, as you know, my aunt was very ill. The poor woman only just survived."

"No, you were quite right not to come. What good would it have done?" Tristana replied, instantly recovering her composure. "Such a sorry sight would have broken your heart. But it's over now. I'm better and getting used to the idea of having only one leg."

"What does that matter, my love?" said Horacio, in order to say something.

"Well, we'll see. I haven't yet tried to walk on crutches. The first day will be difficult, but I'll get used to it. I'll have to."

"It's all a question of habit. Naturally, you won't look quite so elegant to begin with … although, of course, you could never be anything but elegant—"

"No, please. Such empty adulation really isn't right between us. A few compliments, of a charitable nature, fine, but—"

"Your most important qualities, grace, wit, intelligence, remain, needless to say, undiminished as do the charm of your face, the admirable proportions of your body—"

"Shhh," said Tristana gravely, "I am a sedentary beauty now … a woman with only half a body, an upper body, nothing more."

"How can you say 'nothing more,' when the body in question is so very beautiful? Then there is your peerless intelligence, which will always make of you a creature of infinite charm."

Horacio was scouring his mind for all the flowers one can throw at a woman who now has only one leg. They weren't hard to find, but once he had heaped the wretched invalid with them, he had nothing more to add. Slightly embarrassed, an embarrassment he himself barely noticed, he said, "And I love you and will always love you just the same."

"Yes, I know that," she replied, confirming the very thing she was just beginning to doubt.

The conversation continued in the most affectionate terms, but never achieved the tone and texture of genuine trust. In the very first moments, Tristana felt immediate disappointment. This man was not the same man who had been erased from her memory by distance, and whose image she had then laboriously reconstructed with all the force of her creative faculties. He seemed to her rough and vulgar, his face devoid of intelligence, and as for his ideas, they struck her as extraordinarily banal! From Señó Juan's lips there emerged only the kind of commiserative remarks one would offer any patient, albeit clothed in a kind of friendly tenderness. And anything he said about the constancy of his love was clearly an artifice painstakingly built out of compassion.

Meanwhile, shod in silent slippers, so that they would not hear his footsteps, Don Lope paced restlessly about the house and every now and then went over to the door in case anything should happen that required his intervention. Since spying was repugnant to his dignity, he did not put his ear to the door; however, on orders from her master, on her own initiative, and out of a desire to pry, Saturna put her ear to the crack left open for that purpose and was able to catch a little of what the lovers were saying. Calling her out into the corridor, Don Lope plied her with urgent questions.

"Tell me, has marriage been mentioned?"

"I've heard nothing that suggested they might marry," said Saturna. "Plenty about love and loving each other always, and so on, but—"

"Not a word about sacred bonds, though. As I said, it's over. How could it be otherwise? How could he keep his promise to a woman who is going to have to walk on crutches? Nature will out. That's what I say. Lots of talk, lots of high-flown words, but no substance. When it comes to hard facts, all that verbiage gets swept away like so many dead leaves and nothing is left. Anyway, Saturna, that's all to the good and precisely as I hoped. Let's see what the girl does next. Keep listening out for any formal future commitment."

The diligent servant returned to her listening post but was unable to hear much more because the two young people were talking so quietly. Finally, Horacio proposed bringing the visit to an end.

"If it was up to me," he said, "I would stay with you until tomorrow and the day after tomorrow too, but I have to bear in mind that, in allowing me to see you, Don Lope is acting with enormous generosity and high-mindedness, which does him honor and obliges me not to abuse that generosity. Should I leave now, do you think? I'll do as you think fit. But I hope that if my visits are not too long, then he will permit me to come every day."

Tristana agreed with her friend, who withdrew, having first kissed her tenderly and reiterated the affection which, although far from lukewarm, was taking on an increasingly fraternal tone. Tristana watched his departure quite calmly, and as they said goodbye, she arranged to have her first painting lesson with him the following day, which hugely pleased the artist, who, as he left the room, came across Don Lope loitering in the corridor and, going straight over to him, greeted him respectfully. They went into the aging gallant's room and there spoke of things which, to Don Lope, seemed highly significant.

For the moment, the painter said nothing that hinted at marriage plans. He showed intense interest in Tristana, deep pity for her state, and a discreet degree of love, a discretion that Don Lope interpreted as delicacy on Horacio's part or, rather, a feeling of repugnance at the idea of breaking off their relationship too brusquely, which, given Señorita Reluz's sad situation, would have been an act of rank inhumanity. Finally, Horacio was keen to give the interest he felt for Tristana a markedly positivist character. Having learned from Saturna that Don Lope was afflicted by certain financial difficulties, Horacio made a suggestion that proud, dignified Don Lope could not accept.

"Look, my friend," he said in friendly fashion, "I ... and I hope you don't think I'm speaking out of turn ... I have certain duties toward Tristana. She's an orphan. All those who love and esteem her as they should have an obligation to look after her. It doesn't seem right to me that you should have a monopoly on the joy of being able to help the invalid. You would be doing me a considerable favor, for which I will be eternally grateful, if you would allow me to—"

"What? Please, Señor Díaz, don't make me blush. Allow you to do what?"

"Take it as you wish, sir, but what do you mean? That it would be indelicate of me to propose that I pay for Tristana's medical care? Well, you would be quite wrong to think that. Accept my proposal and then we can be even better friends."

"Better friends, Señor Díaz? Better friends once you have established that I have no shame!"

"Please, Don Lope!"

"Don Horacio, that's enough."

"All right, why then shouldn't I make a present to my young

friend of a better-quality organ, the best of its kind, along with a complete library of music, including studies, easy pieces, and concertos, and, finally, that I pay for her music teacher?"

"Now that I can accept. You see how reasonable I am. You may give the organ and the music, but I cannot allow you to pay for the lessons."

"Why not?"

"Because the gift of an organ can be seen as a proof of affections past or present, but I've never heard of anyone making a gift of music lessons."

"Don Lope, why these subtle distinctions?"

"Soon you'll be suggesting that you pay for her clothes and tell her what food to eat...and that, quite frankly, seems insulting to me...unless you were to come to me with certain proposals and aims."

Seeing where he was going, Horacio tried to change the subject slightly.

"My proposal is that she should learn a skill in which she can shine and find an outlet for all the creative fluid that must have accumulated in her nervous system, all the treasures of artistic passion and noble ambition filling her soul."

"Well, if that's what you are proposing, I am perfectly capable of doing the same. I may not be rich, but I have enough money to open up for Tristana whatever paths to glory are available to a poor little cripple. To be honest, I thought that you..."

Wanting to draw from Horacio a categorical statement and seeing that he was getting nowhere with these oblique tactics, he attacked head-on.

"I thought that, in coming here, you were intending to marry her."

"Marry! Oh, no," said Horacio, caught momentarily off guard by that sudden blow, but immediately recovering. "Tristana is an irreconcilable enemy of matrimony. Didn't you know?"

"No, I didn't."

"Oh, yes, she loathes it. Perhaps she sees more keenly than we do;

perhaps her perspicacious gaze or perhaps a certain instinct for divination given only to superior women, can see the way society is going more clearly than we can."

"Yes, perhaps. These spoiled, capricious girls do tend to be far-sighted. Anyway, Señor Díaz, we accept the gift of the organ, but nothing else. We are duly grateful, but we cannot accept the rest for decorum's sake."

"It's agreed though," said Horacio as he was about to leave, "that I will spend a little time with her each day painting."

"Yes, once she's out of bed, because she can't paint while she's still in bed."

"No, of course, but in the meantime, I can come—"

"Oh, yes, to talk to her and distract her. You can tell her about your lovely estate."

"Oh, no," said Horacio, frowning. "She doesn't like the country, or gardening, or Nature, or chickens, or the quiet, obscure life, all of which I adore. I'm very earthbound, very practical, whereas she's a dreamer, with wings of such extraordinary power that she can fly up into endless space."

"Quite so," said Don Lope, shaking his hand. "Well, come and visit whenever you wish, Señor Díaz. You'll always be welcome."

He accompanied him to the door, then went back to his room, gleefully rubbing his hands and saying to himself, "Incompatibility, complete and utter incompatibility, insurmountable differences."

27

DON LOPE noticed that his invalid seemed slightly stunned after Horacio's visit. Tristana, in response to the crafty old man's questions, said frankly, "How that man has changed! He's a different person, and I can't help remembering how he used to be."

"Has he lost or gained in the transformation?"

"Oh, he's definitely lost, at least for the moment."

"He seems a nice enough fellow, though, and he clearly cares about you. He offered to pay your medical expenses, but I refused, of course. I mean, imagine..."

Tristana blushed scarlet.

"And he's not the sort," added Don Lope, "who, when he stops loving a woman, simply leaves without saying goodbye. No, no, he seems very attentive and sensitive. He's going to buy you a new harmonium, an organ, a really good one, plus all the music you could possibly need. I accepted that offer, well, it seemed imprudent to turn him down. In short, he's a good man and he feels sorry for you. He realizes that, in your position, having lost your leg, you need to be pampered and surrounded with distractions and things to do and, like the kind, sincere friend he is, he will, first of all, be giving you a few little painting lessons."

Tristana said nothing, but all day she felt sad. Her interview with Horacio on the following afternoon was rather chilly. The painter could not have been more amiable, but he spoke not one word of love. Don Lope entered the room unannounced and joined in the conversation, which was entirely about artistic matters. When he urged Horacio to talk about the joys of life in Villajoyosa, the painter spoke at length on the subject, which, contrary to Don Lope's belief, seemed to please Tristana. She listened intently to his descriptions of that pleasant existence and of the pure delights of domesticity in the heart of the country. A metamorphosis had doubtless taken place in her heart after the mutilation of her body, and what she had once despised now presented itself to her as the smiling prospect of a new world.

On subsequent visits, Horacio skillfully avoided all reference to the delightful life that was now his most ardent passion. He also revealed himself to be indifferent to art, saying that he felt no interest now in glory and in laurels. And when he said this—which was a faithful reproduction of the ideas expressed in his letters from Villajoyosa—he noticed that Tristana seemed not at all displeased. On the contrary, and much to Horacio's astonishment, for his memory still bore the indelible imprint of the exalted ideas with which his lover had filled her letters, she sometimes appeared to share his view and to look with equal disdain on artistic enterprises and successes.

When she was finally allowed to leave her bed, the narrow room in which the poor invalid spent her hours stuck in an armchair was transformed into an artist's studio. Horacio's patience and solicitude as a teacher knew no bounds, but a strange thing happened: not only did Tristana seem rather uninterested in the art of Apelles; her aptitude too, so evident months before, waned and disappeared, doubtless due to a lack of confidence. Horacio could not believe it, remembering how effortlessly his pupil had understood and manipulated color; and, in the end, to their mutual amazement, both of them began to lose interest and grow bored, either postponing their lessons or cutting them short. After only a few days of such attempts, they barely painted at all, but spent the time talking, until conversation languished too, as it does between people who have said all they have to say to each other and are reduced to speaking only of the ordinary, everyday things of life.

When Tristana tried walking on crutches, her first attempt at that strange system of locomotion was an occasion for much laughter and joking.

"It's quite impossible," she said cheerily, "for anyone to walk elegantly on crutches. However hard I try, I will never be able to skip along on these sticks. I'll be like one of those crippled women who beg for alms at the door of the church. Not that it matters. I will simply have to accept it!"

Horacio proposed sending her a wheelchair so that she could take a turn outdoors. She thanked him for the gift, which duly arrived two days later, although she did not use it for another three or four months. Saddest of all, though, were Horacio's frequent absences. His withdrawal was so slow and gradual that it went almost unnoticed. He began by missing a day, saying that he had various urgent errands to run; the next week, he played truant twice; then three times, then five, and finally no one even bothered to count the days he missed but only the days on which he appeared. Tristana did not seem put out by these absences; she always received him affectionately and watched him leave without apparent sadness. She never asked him why he had not come, still less told him off. Another circumstance worthy of note was the fact that they never spoke about the past: that particular novel, they both seemed to agree, was over and done with, doubtless because it seemed so improbable and false, rather like the books we were mad about in our youth and which, in our maturity, seem somewhat paltry.

With her first music and organ lessons, Tristana emerged almost abruptly, as if by magic, from the spiritual stagnation into which she had sunk. It was like a sudden resurrection, full of life, enthusiasm, and passion, an affirmation of Señorita Reluz's true nature, revealing in her, in the first flush of that new experience, a marvelous talent. Her teacher was a small, affable man endowed with phenomenal patience, so practiced as a teacher and so adept at communicating his methods that he could have made an organist out of a deaf-mute. Under his intelligent guidance, Tristana quickly overcame any initial difficulties, to the surprise and excitement of all who witnessed that miracle. Don Lope was stunned and filled with admiration, and when Tristana pressed down the keys, eliciting from them the sweetest of chords, the poor gentleman waxed positively sentimental, like a grandfather whose sole purpose in life is to spoil the grandchildren on whom he dotes. Her teacher soon added a few notions about harmony to the lessons about mechanisms, fingering, and sight-reading, and it was amazing to see how easily the young woman absorbed these difficult concepts. It was as if she knew the rules before they were revealed to her; she leapt ahead, and whatever she learned remained deeply engraved on her mind. Her diminutive teacher, a devout Christian, who spent his life going from choir to choir and from chapel to chapel, playing solemn masses, funerals, and novenas, saw in his pupil an example of God's favor, of artistic and religious predestination.

"The girl's a genius," he said, gazing at her admiringly, "and sometimes she seems almost a saint."

"Saint Cecilia!" cried Don Lope gaily, his voice almost breaking. "What a daughter, what a woman, what a divinity!"

Horacio could barely conceal his emotion when he heard Tristana playing music of a liturgical nature or a fugue, shaping each musical phrase with astonishing skill; he was hard put to hide his tears, embarrassed to be shedding them. When Tristana, aflame with religious inspiration, immersed herself in the music, translating that grave instrument into the language of her very soul, she was unaware of anyone and oblivious to her small but fervent audience. Emotion and the expression of that emotion absorbed her entirely; her face became transfigured, taking on a celestial beauty; her soul abandoned earthly things in order to be rocked in the vaporous breast of the sweetest of ideals. One day, when her kindly teacher heard her improvising with unusual grace and boldness, his admiration reached new heights for the ease with which she modulated her playing, shifted keys, and generally revealed a knowledge of harmony he had never taught her, as if she were possessed of a mysterious divinatory power, given only to certain privileged souls, for whom art holds no secrets. From that day on, her teacher attended the lessons with an interest that went beyond the purely educational, pouring all his five senses into his pupil, as if she were a much-adored only child. The aging musician and the aging gallant sat in ecstasy before the invalid, and while one, with paternal love, showed her the arcane secrets of the art, the other revealed his pure and tender feelings through sighs and the occasional passionate look. Once the lesson was over, Tristana would take a turn about the room on her crutches, and Don Lope and the other old man both felt, as they watched her, that Saint Cecilia herself could not have moved or walked in any other way.

At around this time, that is, when Tristana was making these leaps of progress, Horacio's visits again became more frequent, then suddenly grew notably less so. With the arrival of summer, two whole weeks went by without a visit from him, but when he did come, Tristana, to please and amuse him, would favor him with a performance; he would sit alone in the darkest corner of the room listening, in profound, trancelike concentration, to her wonderful playing, his eyes fixed on some indeterminate point in space, while his soul wandered free in those regions where dream and reality mingle. And Tristana was so absorbed by that art, which she had so eagerly cultivated, that she did not and could not think of anything else. Each day she wanted more and better music. Her mind was in the grip of perfection, which held her fascinated. Oblivious to what was happening in the outside world, her isolation became complete, absolute. One day, Horacio went to see her and left without her even realizing he had been there.

That afternoon, when no one was expecting it, he set off for Villajoyosa, as it was said that his aunt, who was still living there, was close to death. And it was true, for three days after her nephew arrived, Doña Trini closed the heavy gates of her eyes never to open them again. Shortly afterwards, at the beginning of autumn, Horacio fell ill, although not gravely so. Friendly letters passed between him and Tristana and even Don Lope, and these continued to come and go every two or three weeks, following the same route taken by the incendiary letters once written by Señó Juan and Paquita de

Rimini. Tristana wrote hers very quickly and hurriedly, topping and tailing them with only polite expressions of friendship. Under the influence of one of those inspirations that fills the mind with a profound and true knowledge of things, Tristana believed, as firmly as one believes in the light from the sun, that she would never see Horacio again. And so it was. One November morning, a grave-faced Don Lope entered her room, and in a tone that was neither joyful nor sad, as if he were merely commenting on the weather, he gave her the news coolly and tersely.

"Did you hear? Our Don Horacio is getting married."

28

THE AGING gallant thought Tristana looked slightly taken aback when she received this cup of poison, but she so quickly and confidently regained her composure that Don Lepe could not with any certainty establish his captive's state of mind after this definitive end to her wild passion. Like someone plunging into a tranquil ocean, she leapt into the *mare magnum* of music and spent hours there, now diving down to the depths, now bobbing gracefully up to the surface, completely out of touch with human life and with certain ideas that still tormented her. She never mentioned Horacio again, and although the painter continued to write her the occasional friendly letter, Don Lope was the one who read and responded to them. He was careful not to talk to Tristana about her former adoring lover, and despite all his wisdom and experience, he never knew for sure if Tristana's sad, serene attitude concealed either disappointment or a sense that she had been profoundly wrong to feel so disappointed with the Horacio who came back into her life. But how could Don Lope know this, when she herself did not?

On fine winter afternoons, she went out in the wheelchair, with Saturna pushing. One of the most marked characteristics of the new Señorita Reluz was a complete absence of vanity: She took little care over her appearance and dressed very simply in a shawl and silk head scarf; however, she was still always well shod and frequently quarreled with the shoemaker over any discomfort caused by her one boot. It always struck her as odd having only one shoe to wear. The years would pass, and she never could accustom herself to not seeing the boot or shoe for her right foot.

A year after the operation, her face had grown so thin that to many of those who had known her when she was well, she was now barely recognizable as a wheelchair-bound invalid. She was only twenty-five but looked forty. The wooden leg, with which she was fitted two months after her flesh-and-blood leg had been taken from her, was the finest of its kind, but she could not get used to walking on it with only a stick for support. She preferred to use crutches, even though these made her hunch up her shoulders, thus spoiling the elegant beauty of her neck and upper body. She took to spending her afternoons in the church and, to facilitate that innocent pastime, Don Lope moved from the top of Paseo de Santa Engracia to Paseo del Obelisco, where there were four or five churches within easy reach, nice, modern ones, as well as the parish church of Chamberí. This change of abode suited Don Lope too, since he saved a little money on rent, money that came in handy for other expenses in these calamitous times. Most striking of all was that Tristana's liking for the church communicated itself to her former tyrant, and without the latter even noticing, he began spending pleasant hours in the church of the Servants of the Holy Sacrament, of Our Lady of Life Reparatrice, and of St. Fermin, attending novenas and expositions of the Blessed Sacrament. By the time Don Lope had noticed this new stage in his old-man's habits, he was in no condition to be able to appreciate the oddness of this change. His understanding grew clouded; his body aged with terrible speed; he dragged his feet like an octogenarian, and his head and hands shook. In the end, such was Tristana's enthusiasm for the peace of the church, for the serenity of the services and the chatter of the other regular attendees, all of them devout women, that she reduced the number of hours she devoted to music in order to spend more time in religious contemplation. Like Don Lope, she did not notice this new metamorphosis, which happened in slow stages; and if, at first, she felt only a liking for the church, rather than religious zeal, if her visits were, initially, what one might call acts of pious dilettantism, they soon became acts of genuine piety, and by barely noticeable degrees, these were joined by the Catholic practices of mass, penance, and communion.

And since good Don Lope lived only through and for her, reflecting her sentiments and plagiarizing her ideas, he, too, gradually became immersed in that life, from which his sad old age drew a childish consolation. Occasionally, in moments of lucidity that resembled brief awakenings from a troubled sleep, he would cast an interrogative eye over himself and think, "Is it really me, Lope Garrido, doing these things? I must be senile, yes, senile. The man in me has died, my whole being has been gradually dying, beginning with the present, and advancing, as it dies, toward the past, until nothing is left but the child. Yes, I'm a child, and I think and live as a child. I can see it in this young woman's kindness toward me. I spoiled her, and now she spoils me."

As for Tristana, would this be her final metamorphosis? Or perhaps this change was purely external, and inside there still survived the remarkable unity of her passion for the ideal. The perfect, beautiful being whom she had loved, having constructed him out of materials drawn from reality, had vanished with the reappearance of the person who had been the genesis of that intellectual creation; but the type, in all his essential, faultless beauty, survived intact in the mind of the young invalid. If she was capable of changing her way of loving him, that embodiment of all perfections could also change. First he was a man, then he became God, the beginning and end of all things.

Three years had passed since the operation so skillfully carried out by Miquis and his friend, and Señorita Reluz, without neglecting music entirely, now regarded it with scorn, as an inferior thing of little value. She spent the afternoon in the church of the Servants of the Holy Sacrament, seated on a pew, which, given the fixity and constancy with which she occupied it, appeared to belong to her. Her crutches, propped up beside her, kept her grim company. In the end, the nuns made friends with her, and this resulted in Tristana becoming more involved in the life of the church. For example, on solemn occasions, Tristana would sometimes play the organ, to the joy of the nuns and the whole congregation. The "cripple lady" became a popular figure among those who assiduously attended services morning and evening, and the acolytes already considered her part of the fabric of the building and, indeed, the institution.

29

DON LOPE did not get the lonely, solitary old age he so richly deserved as a fitting conclusion to a life of dissipation and vice, because his relatives saved him from the terrible poverty threatening him. Without the help of his cousins the Señoras de Garrido Godoy, who lived in Jaén, and without the largesse of his nephew Don Primitivo de Acuña, the archdeacon of Baeza, that gallant in decline would have had to beg for alms or deliver his noble bones to the poorhouse. Even though those hysterical, old-fashioned, God-fearing spinsters believed their egregious relative to be a monster, or, rather, a devil let loose upon the world, blood outweighed the bad opinion they had of him, and in a modest way, they helped him in his poverty. As for the good archdeacon, on a visit to Madrid, he tried to obtain from his uncle certain concessions of a moral order; the two men conferred. Don Lope heard what his nephew had to say with growing indignation, and the cleric left feeling utterly downhearted. And nothing more was said of the matter. More time passed, and five years after Tristana's illness, the cleric returned to the fray, trusting in the persuasive power of some new arguments.

"Uncle, you have spent your life offending against God, and the most infamous, most ignominious of those offenses is your criminal union with—"

"But we no longer—"

"That doesn't matter. You and she will both go to hell and all your good intentions now will be worth nothing."

In short, the archdeacon wanted them to marry. How ludicrous, what a terrible irony, given the individual we are dealing with here, Don Lope, a man of radical, dissolute ideas!

"I may be in my dotage," said he, drawing himself up with some difficulty onto the tips of his toes, "I may have been reduced once more to being a snotty-nosed brat, but, please, Primitivo, don't treat me like an imbecile."

The good cleric set out his plans very simply. He was not asking, he was blackmailing. Here's how.

"Your devout cousins," he said, "are offering, if you will fall into line and bow to the commandments of divine law...they are offering, I repeat, to transfer to you their two estates in Arjonilla, which would mean that you could live comfortably for however many more days the Lord sees fit to grant you, as well as being able to bequeath to your widow—"

"My widow!"

"Yes, because your cousins—quite rightly—require you to marry."

Don Lope burst out laughing, not at this extravagant proposal but at himself. The deal was done. How could he reject their proposition when, by accepting it, he would be safeguarding Tristana's existence after his death?

Yes, the deal was done. Who would have thought it? Don Lope, who had lately learned how to make the sign of the cross over forehead and mouth, never ceased now to cross himself. In short, they married, and when they emerged from the church, Don Lope was still not convinced that he had truly abjured his beloved doctrine of bachelorhood. Contrary to his expectations, Tristana had no objections to the absurd plan. She accepted it with indifference; indeed, she had come to regard all earthly things with utter disdain. She barely noticed that she had been married off, that a few brief formulaic words had made her Don Lope's legitimate wife, filing her away in one of society's honorable pigeonholes. She felt nothing, accepting it as something imposed on her by the outside world, like having to register your address with the town hall, pay your taxes, or comply with police regulations.

Thanks to the improvement in his fortunes, Don Lope was able to rent a larger house in Paseo del Obelisco, which had a courtyard-cum-garden. Under this new regimen, the old rake revived; he seemed less senile, less slow-witted, and as he neared the end of his life, he felt stirring inside him—quite how or why he did not know—tendencies he had never known before, the obsessions and longings of a placid bourgeois gentleman. He had hitherto been ignorant of the urgent need to plant a tree, not stopping until he had achieved his desire, until he saw that the plant had taken root and grown fresh new leaves. And while his lady wife was at church praying, he—his religious enthusiasms having already somewhat waned—spent that time taking care of the six hens and the one arrogant cockerel he had in his courtyard. What delight, what excitement, going to see if the hens had laid an egg and, if so, how large, and then preparing the clutch of eggs that would become chicks, which, when they hatched out, were just adorable, so bold and eager to live life to the full! Don Lope was beside himself with contentment, and Tristana shared his excitement. At around that time, she took up a new hobby, that preeminent branch of the culinary arts: cake-making. A skillful teacher taught her how to make a few different sorts of cake, and she made them so well, so very well, that Don Lope, after sampling them, licked his fingers and praised God. Were they happy, the two of them? Perhaps.

TRANSLATOR'S ACKNOWLEDGMENTS

I would like, as ever, to thank both Annella McDermott for all her help and advice, and my husband, Ben Sherriff, who is always my first reader.

TITLES IN SERIES

For a complete list of titles, visit www.nyrb.com or write to:
Catalog Requests, NYRB, 435 Hudson Street, New York, NY 10014

J.R. ACKERLEY Hindoo Holiday*
J.R. ACKERLEY My Dog Tulip*
J.R. ACKERLEY My Father and Myself*
J.R. ACKERLEY We Think the World of You*
HENRY ADAMS The Jeffersonian Transformation
RENATA ADLER Pitch Dark*
RENATA ADLER Speedboat*
CÉLESTE ALBARET Monsieur Proust
DANTE ALIGHIERI The Inferno
DANTE ALIGHIERI The New Life
KINGSLEY AMIS The Alteration*
KINGSLEY AMIS Girl, 20*
KINGSLEY AMIS The Green Man*
KINGSLEY AMIS Lucky Jim*
KINGSLEY AMIS The Old Devils*
KINGSLEY AMIS One Fat Englishman*
WILLIAM ATTAWAY Blood on the Forge
W.H. AUDEN (EDITOR) The Living Thoughts of Kierkegaard
W.H. AUDEN W.H. Auden's Book of Light Verse
ERICH AUERBACH Dante: Poet of the Secular World
DOROTHY BAKER Cassandra at the Wedding*
DOROTHY BAKER Young Man with a Horn*
J.A. BAKER The Peregrine
S. JOSEPHINE BAKER Fighting for Life*
HONORÉ DE BALZAC The Human Comedy: Selected Stories*
HONORÉ DE BALZAC The Unknown Masterpiece *and* Gambara*
MAX BEERBOHM Seven Men
STEPHEN BENATAR Wish Her Safe at Home*
FRANS G. BENGTSSON The Long Ships*
ALEXANDER BERKMAN Prison Memoirs of an Anarchist
GEORGES BERNANOS Mouchette
ADOLFO BIOY CASARES Asleep in the Sun
ADOLFO BIOY CASARES The Invention of Morel
CAROLINE BLACKWOOD Corrigan*
CAROLINE BLACKWOOD Great Granny Webster*
NICOLAS BOUVIER The Way of the World
MALCOLM BRALY On the Yard*
MILLEN BRAND The Outward Room*
SIR THOMAS BROWNE Religio Medici and Urne-Buriall*
JOHN HORNE BURNS The Gallery
ROBERT BURTON The Anatomy of Melancholy
CAMARA LAYE The Radiance of the King
GIROLAMO CARDANO The Book of My Life
DON CARPENTER Hard Rain Falling*
J.L. CARR A Month in the Country*
BLAISE CENDRARS Moravagine
EILEEN CHANG Love in a Fallen City

* *Also available as an electronic book.*

GABRIEL GARCÍA MÁRQUEZ Clandestine in Chile: The Adventures of Miguel Littín
ALAN GARNER Red Shift*
WILLIAM H. GASS In the Heart of the Heart of the Country: And Other Stories*
WILLIAM H. GASS On Being Blue: A Philosophical Inquiry*
THÉOPHILE GAUTIER My Fantoms
JEAN GENET Prisoner of Love
ÉLISABETH GILLE The Mirador: Dreamed Memories of Irène Némirovsky by Her Daughter*
JOHN GLASSCO Memoirs of Montparnasse*
P.V. GLOB The Bog People: Iron-Age Man Preserved
NIKOLAI GOGOL Dead Souls*
EDMOND AND JULES DE GONCOURT Pages from the Goncourt Journals
PAUL GOODMAN Growing Up Absurd: Problems of Youth in the Organized Society*
EDWARD GOREY (EDITOR) The Haunted Looking Glass
JEREMIAS GOTTHELF The Black Spider*
A.C. GRAHAM Poems of the Late T'ang
WILLIAM LINDSAY GRESHAM Nightmare Alley*
EMMETT GROGAN Ringolevio: A Life Played for Keeps
VASILY GROSSMAN An Armenian Sketchbook*
VASILY GROSSMAN Everything Flows*
VASILY GROSSMAN Life and Fate*
VASILY GROSSMAN The Road*
OAKLEY HALL Warlock
PATRICK HAMILTON The Slaves of Solitude
PATRICK HAMILTON Twenty Thousand Streets Under the Sky
PETER HANDKE Short Letter, Long Farewell
PETER HANDKE Slow Homecoming
ELIZABETH HARDWICK The New York Stories of Elizabeth Hardwick*
ELIZABETH HARDWICK Seduction and Betrayal*
ELIZABETH HARDWICK Sleepless Nights*
L.P. HARTLEY Eustace and Hilda: A Trilogy*
L.P. HARTLEY The Go-Between*
NATHANIEL HAWTHORNE Twenty Days with Julian & Little Bunny by Papa
ALFRED HAYES In Love*
ALFRED HAYES My Face for the World to See*
PAUL HAZARD The Crisis of the European Mind: 1680–1715*
GILBERT HIGHET Poets in a Landscape
RUSSELL HOBAN Turtle Diary*
JANET HOBHOUSE The Furies
HUGO VON HOFMANNSTHAL The Lord Chandos Letter*
JAMES HOGG The Private Memoirs and Confessions of a Justified Sinner
RICHARD HOLMES Shelley: The Pursuit*
ALISTAIR HORNE A Savage War of Peace: Algeria 1954–1962*
GEOFFREY HOUSEHOLD Rogue Male*
WILLIAM DEAN HOWELLS Indian Summer
BOHUMIL HRABAL Dancing Lessons for the Advanced in Age*
DOROTHY B. HUGHES The Expendable Man*
RICHARD HUGHES A High Wind in Jamaica*
RICHARD HUGHES In Hazard*
RICHARD HUGHES The Fox in the Attic (The Human Predicament, Vol. 1)*
RICHARD HUGHES The Wooden Shepherdess (The Human Predicament, Vol. 2)*
INTIZAR HUSAIN Basti*
MAUDE HUTCHINS Victorine

OLIVIA MANNING Fortunes of War: The Levant Trilogy*

OLIVIA MANNING School for Love*

JAMES VANCE MARSHALL Walkabout*

GUY DE MAUPASSANT Afloat

GUY DE MAUPASSANT Alien Hearts*

JAMES MCCOURT Mawrdew Czgowchwz*

WILLIAM MCPHERSON Testing the Current*

DAVID MENDEL Proper Doctoring: A Book for Patients and Their Doctors*

HENRI MICHAUX Miserable Miracle

JESSICA MITFORD Hons and Rebels

JESSICA MITFORD Poison Penmanship*

NANCY MITFORD Frederick the Great*

NANCY MITFORD Madame de Pompadour*

NANCY MITFORD The Sun King*

NANCY MITFORD Voltaire in Love*

MICHEL DE MONTAIGNE Shakespeare's Montaigne; translated by John Florio*

HENRY DE MONTHERLANT Chaos and Night

BRIAN MOORE The Lonely Passion of Judith Hearne*

BRIAN MOORE The Mangan Inheritance*

ALBERTO MORAVIA Agostino*

ALBERTO MORAVIA Boredom*

ALBERTO MORAVIA Contempt*

JAN MORRIS Conundrum*

JAN MORRIS Hav*

PENELOPE MORTIMER The Pumpkin Eater*

ÁLVARO MUTIS The Adventures and Misadventures of Maqroll

L.H. MYERS The Root and the Flower*

NESCIO Amsterdam Stories*

DARCY O'BRIEN A Way of Life, Like Any Other

YURI OLESHA Envy*

IONA AND PETER OPIE The Lore and Language of Schoolchildren

IRIS OWENS After Claude*

RUSSELL PAGE The Education of a Gardener

ALEXANDROS PAPADIAMANTIS The Murderess

BORIS PASTERNAK, MARINA TSVETAYEVA, AND RAINER MARIA RILKE Letters, Summer 1926

CESARE PAVESE The Moon and the Bonfires

CESARE PAVESE The Selected Works of Cesare Pavese

LUIGI PIRANDELLO The Late Mattia Pascal

JOSEP PLA The Gray Notebook

ANDREY PLATONOV The Foundation Pit

ANDREY PLATONOV Happy Moscow

ANDREY PLATONOV Soul and Other Stories

J.F. POWERS Morte d'Urban*

J.F. POWERS The Stories of J.F. Powers*

J.F. POWERS Wheat That Springeth Green*

CHRISTOPHER PRIEST Inverted World*

BOLESŁAW PRUS The Doll*

ALEXANDER PUSHKIN The Captain's Daughter*

QIU MIAOJIN Last Words from Montmartre*

RAYMOND QUENEAU We Always Treat Women Too Well

RAYMOND QUENEAU Witch Grass

RAYMOND RADIGUET Count d'Orgel's Ball